TREASURE HUNTERS

Secrets of the Old Church

E. A. HOUSE

EPIC Escape

An Imprint of EPIC Press
abdopublishing.com

Secrets of the Old Church
Treasure Hunters: Book #2

Written by E. A. House

Copyright © 2018 by Abdo Consulting Group, Inc.

Published by EPIC Press™
PO Box 398166
Minneapolis, MN 55439

All rights reserved.

Printed in the United States of America.

International copyrights reserved in all countries.
No part of this book may be reproduced in any form without
written permission from the publisher. EPIC Press™ is trademark
and logo of Abdo Consulting Group, Inc.

Cover design by Laura Mitchell
Images for cover art obtained from iStock and Shutterstock
Edited by Ryan Hume

Library of Congress Cataloging-in-Publication Data
Names: House, E.A., author.
Title: Secrets of the old church/ by E.A. House
Description: Minneapolis, MN : EPIC Press, 2018 | Series: Treasure hunters; #2
Summary: Somewhere in Saint Erasmus's Catholic Church, there's a parish register containing
    a firsthand account of the sinking of the *San Telmo*. To find that ship in honor of their
    murdered aunt, Chris and Carrie first have to find the register. And it turns out that the
    church is supposed to be very haunted.
Identifiers: LCCN 2017949808 | ISBN 9781680768770 (lib. bdg.)
    | ISBN 9781680768916 (ebook)
Subjects: LCSH: Adventure stories—Fiction. | Code and cipher stories—Fiction.
    | Family secrets—Fiction. | Treasure troves—Fiction | Young adult fiction.
Classification: DDC [FIC]—dc23
LC record available at http://lccn.loc.gov/2017949808

For Mom

CHAPTER ONE

MADDISON MCRAE WAS NOT STUPID. CHEERFUL, yes, and often optimistic, and not a perfect straight-A student, but stupid? No. Maddison was not stupid, and Maddison knew a secret when she saw one. Or perhaps more accurately, she knew a secret when people went to great lengths to keep it from her.

Maddison was sitting cross-legged on her bed, flipping through an illustrated collection of Florida urban legends and letting her bowl of cereal slowly turn to mush. Dawn was just breaking over Archer's Grove, Florida, on the last Tuesday in the month of May, and several people might have been murdered over the course of the night. Maddison had been up worrying the whole night because she liked most of those people.

It really just figured, Maddison thought, that she had managed to get mixed up in some sort of secret—if it was a conspiracy or a society or just one of those secrets people kill to keep quiet, Maddison wasn't sure—within one week of moving to a new neighborhood. Back in Fredericksburg she had been the co-founder and only sane member of a paranormal research club and had been locked in a battle of wills with an ex–best friend from kindergarten, and yet most of the time she had been bored. The club had been nothing but lunch meetings and it had taken Maddison an embarrassingly long time to figure out that half the members just wanted an excuse to kiss in dark corners, and Katie had just been generally mean. In Archer's Grove, Maddison had volunteered to help the school secretary with data entry and stumbled into a massive secret that seemed to involve the archives, her father, half the Kingsolver family, and a couple of ghosts.

Maddison was scowling darkly at her book while

trying not to upset the bowl of cereal on her quilt, so she didn't register the sound of a car in the drive until a door slammed, even though she was listening for her dad. Immediately after the door slammed, the screen on the front door made a sound like a cat caught in a rocking chair, then there was a murmured conversation between her parents, a heavy sigh from her mom, and the stairs creaked. All the way up to Maddison's attic room and her open doorway.

"Mads," her dad said, leaning against the doorframe, "cereal on the bed?" He looked rumpled and as though he'd been running his hands through his hair, but he didn't look injured or, you know, dead, and a lot of the worry Maddison had been refusing to admit she was feeling disappeared. It was promptly replaced by the guilty realization that she'd just been caught misbehaving, and when she took a large mouthful of chocolate crispies it was a gesture of defiance. Her dad just smiled at her. Maddison had once seen a character in a book described as having a "wry smile" and she finally had a name to put to what her dad did whenever he caught Maddison doing something she wasn't supposed to and thought she was adorable. It drove Maddison nuts.

"It's . . . so that . . . you'd have to come home to yell at me?" Maddison offered when she'd finished the mouthful of cereal. She was allowed to eat in her bedroom, but she was not supposed to eat things that could spill and ruin upholstery in her room, and cereal with milk was the worst culprit.

"Uh huh," Dr. Kevin McRae said, coming all the way into the room and holding a hand out. Maddison passed him the bowl and he took a large spoonful, then winced.

"I put chocolate milk on them," Maddison admitted guiltily.

"*I can see that,*" her dad gasped, fanning at his mouth as if he'd eaten something hot. "*Gaaah,* that's sweet." He cleared his throat and swallowed a couple of times. "Okay then, now that I've given myself a sugar rush to take the edge off the adrenaline crash—" Maddison had opened her mouth to ask what he meant by *adrenaline crash* when he added, "We need to talk."

Okay, so her dad didn't want his explanation of what happened at the Kingsolver's house to turn into twenty questions. Maddison was still teetering between worried and mad, so all she said was, "You took my cereal so I can't pretend to have my mouth full."

Her dad studied the bowl of soggy cereal for a second, took another spoonful, and then handed it back to Maddison.

"Well I *certainly* didn't do it for my health," he said, and then he softened, a little bit, and added, "Everyone's fine, Mads. Your young man is going to have a magnificently bruised tailbone and his sister is frankly quite terrifying, but nobody died."

"He's *not* my young man," Maddison protested, a half second before she realized this was exactly the right way to convince her father that Chris *was,* and added, "and Chris and Carrie are cousins, not siblings."

"Well they certainly act like siblings," her dad said. "And that's . . . not actually what I wanted to talk to you about, but I did need to reassure you that everyone was fine. I think it would be better for you to call up Carrie and spend an hour or six letting her tell you what happened. That is, when she's worked off the adrenaline enough to call. What I actually need to do," he said, settling himself in Maddison's desk chair, and again sidestepping Maddison's frantic demands for answers, because why would *Carrie* need to work off the adrenaline? Was *everyone* running on frenetic adrenaline right now, except for Maddison, who was going to be in a minute or two if she didn't get some answers?

"I need to tell you a little bit about my past," Maddison's dad said.

Maddison fumbled the cereal bowl directly into her trashcan.

Maddison hadn't gotten into ghosts and aliens and Bigfoot because her dad was a historian. That just made for an easy excuse. She'd gotten into the stuff at the age of eleven because her public library kept the books on the CIA and the history of intelligence agencies right next to the books on ghosts, and ghosts were . . . well, ghosts were safe, as strange as that sounded, or at least safer than what Maddison had actually been worried about at that age. Maddison had really been trying to determine if her dad had been in witness protection.

By the time she was eleven Maddison had known that her dad was hiding something from her. Kevin McRae had a carefully concealed blank spot in his past, one a lot of people didn't ever seem to notice. He would happily share family history and early childhood memories, his wedding photo was proudly displayed on his desk, and he was still in contact with his parents, but nobody knew anything about Kevin McRae from age eighteen to twenty-two. This was, coincidentally, the age during which he ought to have been getting his bachelor's degree from college, and that must have been what he was doing because he had then gotten a doctorate and gone on to teach. And yet not even Dr. McRae's students could tell his daughter with much certainty where he had gone to school; the general impression seemed to be that he'd studied abroad.

There were other things that puzzled Maddison. For one, McRae was her mother's family name, which her father had taken when they married. For another, her father's oldest friendship was with a retired police detective named Gregory Lyndon, who was thirty years older than Maddison's dad and lived halfway across the country. And then there was her dad's very strange behavior over the past months, which had probably started the year before when the Edgewater Maritime Archive started a project with the Archer's Grove State Park. They had wanted to preserve and map out some old ruins in the local state park and had asked Maddison's dad to consult with them on the old Spanish mission hidden somewhere in the park. Maddison's dad loved getting his hands dirty. He regularly volunteered at state and national parks and was a well-regarded expert on the subject of Spanish mission churches. He would even have been paid for his work, and yet he had refused outright. There was something in her dad's past that cast a long, dark shadow over his present, and Maddison was becoming increasingly certain that whatever the secret was it had roots in Archer's Grove.

"You want to tell me about your past," she repeated, in case she hadn't heard right. But there weren't a lot of words that sounded like "past," so unless her dad really wanted to talk about his pants, or his pest, or his . . . pasta . . . ? That was stretching it.

"You don't . . . " Maddison's father started to say, and then the corner of his mouth quirked up. "I was going to say that you don't have to sound so surprised," he said. "But to be brutally fair you *do* have a right to be surprised."

Maddison had never truly thought that pretending to be interested in ghosts would keep her dad from figuring out what she was really worried about, and they'd been in a slightly uncomfortable, unspoken truce for years. Maddison made it very clear that she knew her dad had secrets he wasn't telling the rest of the family, and Maddison's dad steadfastly pretended he wasn't hiding anything. Maddison's mom did a lot of eye rolling but that was easy for her, because Maddison was pretty sure she knew what her husband was hiding.

"You have a giant hole in your life history," Maddison said very fast, so that she could pretend not to have said it if it turned out to be the wrong thing to say.

"I do," her dad said. "And I'm not going to fill it in very much with this, so I apologize in advance." He was sitting in a swivel chair, and he took a moment to spin himself back and forth before he started.

"So, when I was a little older than you, I read this book called *Treasure Island*," he said. "And promptly became enamored with the idea of finding buried treasure. Not so much the treasure at the end, really, as much as the adventuring around, dodging sinister pirates and keeping an eagle eye out for clues. And I was already a history nut, going off to college in

Florida, so it was a bit like I tripped and fell into studying Spanish colonial history."

All of this was new, but none of it was very surprising or worth hiding, and some of this must have shown in Maddison's expression, because her dad sighed. "I know, I'm getting there." He picked up Maddison's pen, the one that had a pink, fluffy pom-pom on the end, and turned it over in his hands. "So, I went away to college. And one of the things about college is that it's so much more open and broader than high school. You meet so many people that you eventually find your niche—I look forward to you discovering that, Mads. And in my case, the niche was treasure hunting."

Maddison blinked.

"Yeah," her dad said. "We spent all our free time looking for treasure—a specific treasure trove, to be exact. It was the early nineties, and the excavating had just started to get interesting with regards to the 1717 Fleet. And *that*," he said, "led me and a couple of friends to spend all our free time looking for the *San Telmo*—it's one of the missing three, and there are

15

some great rumors that it went down around here. We never found the ship," Maddison's dad added, "and I . . . grew out of the whole treasure-hunting thing, but I'm afraid it's in your blood all the same."

"What about Mom?" Maddison asked, instead of what she really wanted to ask, which was *why are you telling me this and what does it mean?*

"Your mother knows all about my dark and sordid past," Maddison's dad said lightly. "And now so do you."

Maddison raised a single eyebrow at him, although it was a slightly wobbly eyebrow.

"Okay, yeah." Her dad pointed the pom-pom end of the pen at her. "I know, Mads. But I *don't* want to tell you. It won't be a fun conversation."

Which was more or less what Maddison had imagined he'd say the many times she rehearsed a confrontation speech and then chickened out at the last minute.

"Oh, I'm *awful* at this," her dad added, and then he squared his hands on his knees and said, "Maddison,

I want you to be careful if you get mixed up in some sort of treasure hunt. Very, *very* careful. There are some nasty, opportunistic people out there and you've got my bullheadedness and drive. And you've got my mind for mystery, I've always been able to see that."

And before Maddison could think of a reply, he had stood up, clapped his hands together, said, "Good talk!" and marched out of the room. Maddison was left to wrestle with a warning that might have been very clear and an explanation that wasn't, but before she could do much thinking about either, Carrie called her. Her father possibly had superpowers, either to see the future or to warp it to his will. Carrie had a shake in her voice that suggested she'd had a very terrible evening, and then she told Maddison about being attacked by a gun-wielding maniac who turned out to have been the person who'd killed her Aunt Elsie, proving that she *had* had a very terrible evening. Maddison told her, in full, what had happened before her father rushed out of the house in a panic the night before, and they both agreed that Mrs. Hadler, school secretary and unexpectedly terrifying person, should never know. Then Carrie hung up and Maddison went to deal with the bowl of cereal in her trash can, wondering just what Chris and Carrie were trying to hide from her. And how much of it her father knew about and was also trying to hide from her.

Chris Kingsolver was beginning to fear for the life of his windowsill. It was a muggy Tuesday evening and Chris had spent the day hollowing out an old book into a secret compartment for hiding his Aunt Elsie's letter. He had, for once in his life, enjoyed the peacefulness, although it was broken by the creeping feeling that he should be doing more research into the mystery his Aunt Elsie had left him, and the nagging sense that he was never going to successfully evade his mom's attempts to get him to find a summer job. His mom had stopped turning every conversation they had into a list of local businesses that were currently hiring, probably because she felt sorry he'd almost gotten shot by a home invader, but had started leaving job applications everywhere instead. She had shoved three applications from her friend's bakery under the door over the course of the day, and Chris actually tried to fill one out, before the facts that he couldn't bake and that the bakery had been the only place Aunt Elsie bought muffins from brought him up short. Job hunting was stressful enough without it reminding him of his aunt.

It had been less than a day since Chris and Carrie had unlocked a hidden box, discovered the secret clue to buried treasure hidden in their Aunt Elsie's notes, and gone up against a gunman who had then admitted he was responsible for murdering their aunt. Chris, at least, was exhausted. What nobody ever told you about getting stuck in an action-adventure movie was how stressful it was, even if you did end up sleeping for a full day afterwards. How Carrie had dug up the stamina to go to work early Wednesday morning Chris couldn't imagine, and why she was climbing through his window again he didn't want to imagine. This time, too, she had her school backpack over one shoulder. It was bulging.

"Carrie," Chris said as the mattress bounced impressively from the weight of her backpack and Chris realized he was lucky she had not dropped a backpack the size of a boulder on his head, "we have a front door."

"So, I did a little research," Carrie said instead of answering.

"A little?" Chris asked, peering into Carrie's backpack. It was stuffed full of books.

"Yeah, I stopped at the library on the way home from work," Carrie said. "This is just what they had on the shelves, I've got a couple of things on hold too."

"Are you sure that's wise?"

"Well," Carrie said, "libraries don't usually—or at least our library doesn't—keep a record of which books a patron checks out after they return them. It's a little safer than *buying* books somewhere, and besides I spend a lot of time there anyway."

Chris was cautiously piling up books on his bedspread. Carrie had a dozen state and local histories stuffed into her backpack, along with a general book on early Spanish settlements in Florida and a pile of things about archeology and treasure hunting. And several maps that looked like she'd printed them off Google. And when, Chris wondered, had Carrie found the time to mark pages with colored sticky notes, or found the time to collect all these different colors of sticky notes?

"Find anything?" he asked.

Carrie sighed. "Soooorta?"

"Oh great," Chris said, and grabbed a pen and piece of paper.

"So," Carrie said, flipping open the book on early Spanish settlements. "First things first. Aunt Elsie found a letter from a deacon that talks about a Father Dominic Gonzalez who saw the wreck. According to this County History"—she dumped a musty book with a fraying cover on Chris's lap and thought for a moment—"and the one in the reference section that I couldn't check out, he would have to have been priest of the Spanish mission Santa Maria de la Mar, because that was the only mission in the area and on the coast. The Mission doesn't exist anymore, but I looked at the history page of every Catholic church in the county that had a website and got lucky." Carrie handed Chris a printed sheet. "And found this."

"*History of Saint Erasmus Catholic Church, 1713 to 2016*," Chris read. "This is the church today?"

"This is the church that sort of absorbed the Santa Maria de la Mar mission and two others and became Saint Erasmus years after the shipwreck," Carrie explained. "Then that church, and most of its records, were moved in the eighteen hundreds, and then again in the early nineties. But if the record *does* survive, this is who will have it."

"And what kind of records are we looking for?" Chris asked. He'd been paging through one of the books on Florida history and stopped on a full-color photo of a hand-drawn map, realizing that Aunt Elsie's note had not indicated what kind of eyewitness account they were looking for, except that if they found a video they were doing it all wrong. Carrie pulled a book on local genealogy out of the pile and handed it over.

"Parish Register?"

"Church record of births, deaths, marriages, and other notable events," Carrie said. "Mrs. Greyson talked my ear off about genealogy research when I checked it out; apparently they're super useful if you're trying to find missing relatives. And before you ask," Carrie added, "yes, I let Mrs. Greyson think I was interested in genealogy. Otherwise she'd have wanted to know why I was checking out so many books on local history, and insisting it's a school project only goes so far."

"Right," Chris said. The sidebar on the printout from Saint Erasmus's website listed the church's weekly events, and there were a lot of them. "So we just have to figure out a way to get into a church that is currently in regular use, find where they keep their oldest and most delicate records, and get a description of the location of the wreck from those records before anyone starts getting suspicious."

"Well," Carrie said mildly, "I never said it was going to be *easy*."

CHAPTER TWO

THEY HAD TO GO IN TO THE POLICE STATION AND give statements the next day, which *shouldn't* have been anything more than a formality. Detective Hermann was simply being careful about getting everyone's stories straight when they weren't all panicking and in the Kingsolvers' living room. And it would have been—Chris was almost embarrassed by how easy it was to recount the disastrous mess on the previous Monday night to a good-natured officer without mentioning the missing locket—but then someone decided it was a good idea to walk Cliff Dodson out right in front of him, and parked the man at the front desk while the officer who was escorting Dodson filled out paperwork.

And even that wouldn't have been too much of a problem—Chris wasn't the type to charge across a police station and attack someone in the name of revenge—except Dodson wouldn't stop looking at *him*. Chris lost track of the questions Officer Jackson was asking him and found himself in a staring contest over her head, and finally Dodson broke first.

"You really don't know about him, do you, kid?" he asked. Officer Jackson looked up and turned to see Dodson, paled, and got quickly to her feet.

"Stay there," she said to Chris, and ducked into the conference room where Detective Hermann was working.

"Don't know about who?" Chris asked as soon as she was out of earshot. The officer filling out the paperwork—probably to transfer Dodson to the county jail—was sure taking his sweet time doing it.

"You should never trust authority figures," Dodson said instead of answering. "Listen kid, you're smarter than I expected but if you can't figure out who's on your side you aren't gonna make it."

"*What?*"

Dodson cast a furtive glance around the room and leaned closer. "You should give up the search, kid," he said in a whisper. "It's gonna get you killed."

"What are you *talking* about?" Chris started to ask in a furious whisper, terrified that Dodson knew about the *San Telmo* and equally terrified that his best chance of finding the person who was behind his aunt's murder was about to clam up. But then Detective Hermann came out of the conference room and marched directly over to the officer filling out paperwork, grabbing him roughly by the elbow. There was a short, furious conversation—Detective Hermann kept his voice too low to be heard but the tone sounded angry and the officer who'd been filling out paperwork went from annoyed at the interruption to shamefaced to horrified in quick succession—and then he escorted Dodson into another room, scowling furiously.

"Idiot," Detective Hermann muttered, half to Chris

and half to himself. "I have no idea what he was *thinking,* putting Dodson in the same room with you."

Chris had a suspicion, but he didn't tell it to Detective Hermann because it wasn't fair—or safe—to tell the police detective that you thought one of the police officers might have been trying to scare you. It was the sort of thing that happened only in bad action movies.

The other thing that often happened in action movies and that was now happening with frustrating frequency in Chris's own life was the horribly complicated juggling of all the different lies Chris had told to different people. His parents knew one version of what had happened on Monday, Maddison knew a more detailed but still different take, and then there was Professor Griffin, who turned up bright and early Wednesday morning to pick up his keys.

He had called and left a message Tuesday afternoon,

apologizing for the inconvenience but explaining that he'd been called in to deal with a minor disaster involving the submersible and would have to delay picking up his keys until Wednesday. Chris had been failing to sleep for fear of nightmares, and his parents had been having a joint panic attack and discussing home security systems over Skype with Carrie's mom and dad, and nobody had heard the phone ring. And then, on Tuesday, nobody had been sure what to tell Professor Griffin, or even if they should, and the end result was their oldest family friend wandering into a minefield with no protective gear.

He'd never actually done that, although there had once been a terrifying day Professor Griffin had waded into a bunch of *stingrays* with no protective gear. Chris couldn't help but be reminded of that incident when Professor Griffin turned up with an offering of carrot and apple muffins.

He looked tired and his hat was on backwards, which was okay with a ball cap but did not work with a captain's hat, and was how Chris knew *Moby* had almost sunk again. Professor Griffin always had three or four different research projects going on at once, and for the past year and a half all three of his projects had involved mapping the sea floor just off the coast. Because of the limits of academic budgets, all three projects had to make due with only one submersible, and a shoddily built one at that—although if you said so to Professor Griffin's face he would fake a fainting fit. *Moby* circled between the three different projects on an intricate schedule that was regularly ruined by the submersible getting lost or stuck somewhere.

Once, *Moby* had been mistaken for a bomb by an overenthusiastic team of Navy Seals doing parachuting drills over the ocean, and only Aunt Elsie's friendship with half of the U.S. Coast Guard Auxiliary had saved the college from getting stormed by a special ops unit. Professor Griffin had ended *that* day with his hat on inside out, so in the grand scheme of things his having it backwards wasn't that bad of a sign.

"So," Professor Griffin said, trading the muffins for the keys and twirling his hat in one hand, "I really must apologize, I had to attend to an unexpected development involving *Moby* and a flotation device and never did get back to you about those keys." He paused and brushed flecks of Styrofoam from his hat. "Never, by the way, leave Ph.D. students alone with expensive equipment when they're sleep deprived," he explained. "The results aren't pretty and they make you leave foreboding messages on answering machines—I didn't mean to traumatize you, by the way."

He was clearly not expecting Chris and both his parents to begin laughing hysterically.

✗ ✗ ✗

"Do you think we should tell him about the letter?" Chris said to Carrie later that afternoon in the municipal park halfway and a bit between their houses and Maddison's.

They were supposed to be meeting Maddison, so they could talk, face to face, about what had happened on Monday, and also to also have a joint freak-out if they needed one. They were in the park because hanging out at home was getting smothering, and Carrie had managed to get her parents and Chris's parents to agree that they were *unlikely* to be attacked in the municipal park. Plus, Maddison had never been.

"And anyway," Chris had pointed out, "the person who was trying to kill us is in police custody, so there's nothing to worry about, right?" His parents had not been reassured and he himself was starting not to believe this—even if Detective Hermann wasn't responsible for Cliff Dodson being able to give Chris that cryptic warning, someone in the police station still was. Did they need to start suspecting the police?

He'd brought the subject up with Carrie, who'd been less than willing to suspect the police and had reminded him that they weren't sure the danger *was* passed, and they were now arguing about the pros and cons of telling Professor Griffin.

"Aunt Elsie said not to trust *anyone*," Carrie reminded him, picking absently at a swath of Spanish moss. Caliban Park was small, but it had a couple of walking trails and just enough trees to give the illusion of wildness, plus when they'd moved the playground from one side of the park to the other and updated it they had not torn down or fenced off the old slide-swings-and-treehouse. It was in this that Carrie and Chris were perched, hiding in the Spanish moss.

"We're going to have to trust someone," Chris pointed out. "If only because we're a little young to go treasure hunting by ourselves. And we don't know anyone else who has access to a boat."

"Oh, I see," Carrie said. "We need to tell the professor because we need his boat."

"Well, we could just tell him we needed to borrow his boat for, I don't know, a school project," Chris suggested sarcastically. "And just happen to find a sunken ship while we're at it—and maybe we'll get lucky and the ship will be run aground somewhere on dry land."

"They make seasickness medication, you know," Carrie said sweetly. "You just have to carry it with you. We live in Florida, you should expect to be exposed to the ocean at any time and be appropriately prepared."

Chris threw a twig at her, because it had only been once and he only ever got seasick on really, really choppy seas.

"It's just that I don't actually lie to people all that much?" Chris tried. "I mean, I'm not perfect and I know that. But . . . " He paused, trying to decide how to put it.

"You're a loveable slacker, not a heartless schemer," Carrie said.

"Yeah—a *what* schemer?"

"Scheming, conniving, etcetera," Carrie said with some venom, so Chris wisely decided to leave the point alone. Sometimes Carrie got teased for being a grade-A perfectionist.

"I just don't like lying to Professor Griffin," he finished. Carrie made a vague agreeing noise and then something Chris had said must have occurred to her, because she gave Chris yet another *liar, liar, pants on fire* look.

"You mean, you don't like lying to *Maddison*," Carrie said, and Chris groaned and nodded. "I don't like lying to her, either," Carrie admitted. "But—you realize how much of an epic tangle you're going to get yourself into if you tell her everything?"

"One that will be worse than the tangle that happens when she finds out all on her own?"

Carrie hissed. At almost the same moment her phone chimed, and she answered it with a chipper, "Hey, Maddison!"

"Yeah, no, we are at the playground at the park, we're just not at the new one," she continued after a minute, as Chris squeaked and blushed as though Maddison had actually caught him lying. He was even trying to politely tamp down his crush, so why had his cheeks not gotten with the program? "It's—do you see the bike trail?" Carrie continued, blissfully unaware of Chris's internal argument. "We're just off the trail by that giant clump of ferns. Yeah—no, it's not haunted. I mean, as far as I know it isn't haunted, we only used to come out here every weekend when we were in elementary school."

"Still, it looks it," Maddison said from beneath

them, and Chris peered over the railing to find her giving one of the faded plastic swings an experimental push. She looked up, saw him, and waved, then trotted over to the treehouse.

"How many spiders are up here?" she asked with one foot on the ladder.

"Chris makes me sweep them all out before he'll come up," Carrie said cheerfully, giving Maddison a hand up. The treehouse was really part of the play set and not in a tree, and it was basically a box, with a simple wooden ladder on one side and a green plastic slide on the other. Chris was sitting along one wall and Carrie, who secretly liked living dangerously, had her back to the slide, which meant she was perfectly placed to pull Maddison up.

"Hey!" Chris protested, shifting over to make room; the treehouse was not built with three teenagers in mind. Maddison's head was brushing the seam in the ceiling and possibly collecting spiders, and Chris's knees were almost touching Carrie's. "I . . . their legs are so *squiggly*," he said. Maddison gave him an understanding grin and settled cross-legged with her back to the ladder, and then they sat there, the three of them, clearly wondering how exactly to broach the subject of what had happened since they'd last met.

"Soooo," Maddison finally said to Carrie. "I did not know you knew your way around guns."

Carrie sighed. Chris snickered. Maddison looked between them and said, "Wait, is this something to do with the handgun Mrs. Hadler has in her desk?"

"Seriously?" Chris demanded. *That was supposed to be a myth!*

"I *told* you," Carrie said. "Mrs. Hadler led a *very* interesting life before she became a school secretary!"

"Well, Dad was impressed," Maddison said, but with a slight hesitation that suggested to Chris that she wasn't sure about bringing her father into this. "And according to him, you made a favorable impression on the police detective."

Carrie groaned.

"But what I want to know," Maddison continued, "is what the heck actually happened that night. I mean,

Dad said it was some guy after the Archive's gold, which—does the Archive even *have* any gold?"

"Couple of gold coins and I think a candlestick or two," Chris said absently. He was trying to give Carrie a significant look with his eyebrows. He wasn't going to get a better chance to tell Maddison. Carrie, of course, was stubbornly refusing to catch his eye. Well then, he'd just have to do it himself.

"Actually," Chris said, while Carrie finally caught his eyes to give him a warning and concerned look. "Um, we might actually have an idea why he was after us? I mean, a better one than the police do."

Carrie grimaced, and then quietly backed herself onto the playground slide and disappeared out of sight.

"Really?" Maddison asked, after a long moment of staring in puzzlement after the suddenly disappearing Carrie. She sounded concerned. Chris didn't blame her; he was concerned too.

"Yeah," Chris said, and then there was nothing for it but to bite the bullet. "So, when our aunt died she left me a letter in . . . in code, and it said that

she wanted us to get something from under the floorboard in her office. That was the box we found last
Monday—it unlocked when we used Carrie's locket
as a key—but we didn't know about that until we
found it."

Maddison nodded, once.

"And," Chris continued, aware that he was waving
his hands around but not sure how to stop, "when we
opened the box there was another letter in it, telling us
that she'd been m-murdered, and that it was because
of the stuff she'd left in the box, which was"—Chris
took another deep breath to try to slow himself down,
because he was doing that nervous thing where he bab-
bled at a hundred miles an hour—"notes she'd been
taking when she was researching the last exhibit she put
together, when she found an actual eyewitness account
of a sunken treasure ship."

Maddison stared at him. Then, very carefully, like
she suspected she knew what the answer was going to
be but hoped she was mistaken, she asked, "Was it the
San Telmo?"

"Yes," Chris admitted, and then watched in horror as Maddison's face crumpled. "I—" he started to say, with no idea how he was going to end that sentence, when Maddison held up a hand. She was fighting back tears—why was she *crying?*—and shaking her head.

"I—I can't . . . right now," she stammered, groping blindly for the open doorway. At some point she had gone *white*. "I'm sorry, Chris," she continued, wiping a hand furiously across her face, and her voice went hard, suddenly. "I need to be somewhere else right now."

If she actually used the ladder she skipped every other rung, before hitting the ground layer of weed-overgrown woodchips with a heavy *thunk* and a gasp that was more about anger than any pain from her landing. And then she didn't bolt, exactly, but stalked away, angry, her back straight. Chris was left gaping.

"Wow," Carrie said quietly into the shocked stillness. Had she really been on the swings this *whole* time? "That went even worse than I thought it would." But she was already climbing up into the treehouse to give Chris a hug, so he could very definitely *not* cry

into her shoulder a bit and have it be an unacknowl-
edged secret.

The problem, when all was said and done—which was
in and of itself the problem, Carrie pointed out, he'd
went and *said* what they'd *done*—was that Chris didn't
know why Maddison was upset. More specifically, he
didn't know if it was the *San Telmo*, the fact that he'd
lied, or some other combination of factors that had her
so upset, and he definitely didn't know how to find
her and fix it. She turned up to work at the school the
next day as usual, and was, Carrie reluctantly informed
Chris after he pestered her all night, perfectly polite, if
a bit withdrawn.

"But that really doesn't mean anything," Carrie
explained from her perch in Chris's open window.
There was a storm blowing in and lightning was
already flashing in the sky, so she needed to get back to
her own house soon. Chris was hiding sulkily under his

covers. "Some girls can be perfectly civil on the surface while privately wanting to stab you to death, and I've only known her for three weeks so I don't know where she falls on that spectrum."

"Okay," Chris sighed mournfully. It was uncomfortably hot under all his blankets, but one sheet just didn't hide you from the world well enough. "I just thought I'd ask."

"You didn't do a bad thing," Carrie said. "You understand that, right? Telling Maddison the truth was the right thing to do—"

"Even if it means she hates me?"

"Honestly, probably especially if it means she hates you," Carrie said. "Now, I need to get inside before I get electrocuted, but I'll be over tomorrow morning and we can do something—"

"About the church," Chris suggested.

"That's a terrible idea," Carrie said. Then she looked at Chris, and the piles of research he'd been doing to keep his mind off Maddison, and sighed. Partly, Chris suspected, because his room was filled with drifting piles of notes and resembled a trailer park after a tornado. "But yeah, we can go look into the church tomorrow."

✗ ✗ ✗

Maddison managed a day and a half of clutching her anger tight to her chest and raging against the unfairness of it all before her dad intervened. It was almost a relief, because raging quietly against someone was *exhausting.* Maddison liked being with people and talking with people and just people in general. She tended to wilt if you left her by herself for too long. A whole day going through the file cabinet marked M, which actually held the student records for last names I and K, and watching everything she said because she was in an enclosed space with the cousin of someone she was furious at (and let's be honest, she was furious with Carrie too) had left her twitchy and irritable and horribly lonely.

Mrs. Hadler, meanwhile, had giant cat's-eye glasses

but perfect twenty-twenty vision when it came to high school students, and she'd given Maddison and Carrie concerned looks over her glasses all day before finally inviting them both to her book group's summer tea on Saturday. Maddison had a micromanaging great-aunt on her mother's side and suspected this was part of a plan to strand her and Carrie in a sea of fluttery old ladies so they *had* to reconcile or die, but there had been no polite way to refuse the offer. Maddison had accepted the invitation with as much grace as possible, managed by a minor miracle not to catch Carrie's eye, and gone home to feel glum and watch movies until her eyes fell out.

She was curled up in the living room eating chocolate crispies dry right out of the box, eyes glued to the climactic fight scene of her third movie of the evening, when her dad came in and sat down next to her with a thump and a weary sigh. Maddison tried very hard to pretend he wasn't there. This was made nearly impossible when he stole the couch blanket out from under her nest of pillows.

Together, they watched a large squid-like creature escape from its ancient enchanted prison and attack the scientists in their tiny, tiny boat. Dramatic music played. The camera wobbled. The secondary love interest was snagged by a tentacle.

"Mads," her dad said over the synthesized sea-monster noises. "What's the matter?"

"Nothing's the matter," Maddison said, far too stubbornly for the comment to be true, and her father sighed and tugged the cereal box out of her hand.

"You have watched five movies over the last two days," he said gently. "And every single one has been the second movie out of a trilogy."

"So?" Maddison asked. On screen, the squid-like creature thrashed and the primary love interest lashed himself to a harpoon, speechifying dramatically.

"So, the second movie of a trilogy is always the one with the darkest ending," her dad said, tossing a handful of chocolate crispies into his mouth and grimacing. "Argh, why do I keep doing that to myself?"

45

"This movie doesn't have *that* dark of an ending," Maddison protested.

"The Colonel is about to be eaten by the tentacle monster," her dad said flatly, and Maddison groaned. He was right, of course. The Colonel *was* about to get eaten by a tentacle monster, not knowing that his best friend had betrayed him to Poseidon for the map to Atlantis or that the duchess had decided to accept his marriage proposal. Maddison fished the remote out from amongst the sofa cushions and hit pause just before the sea nymph revealed her parentage.

"Chris . . . admitted a couple of things to me yesterday," she grumbled.

"And he's secretly a serial killer?"

"No! He . . . he lied to me about why he and Carrie needed to go look through the office last Monday," Maddison said. Her dad raised his eyebrows. "Now that I think about it, I bet Carrie didn't even really lose her necklace," Maddison added. *And that, Maddison,* she told herself guiltily, *was petulant. Even if it was highly manipulative of Carrie.*

"Nah—well, I did see a necklace in a drawer," her dad offered. Maddison was strangely grateful that he didn't try to convince her Chris and Carrie weren't lying. "So who knows if she did? But that isn't enough to make you this angry, Mads."

"They needed to get into the office because their aunt left them a letter telling them to get a box from under the floorboards that apparently had some secret information about the *San Telmo* in it," Maddison said, and was gratified to see her father go briefly blank faced, like he did sometimes when he didn't want to give away anything by reacting. "Chris says his aunt thought she was likely to be murdered for that information," Maddison added. On second thought, her dad might just be having a number of emotions she'd never seen before all show up on his face at once.

"Fudge," he finally said, with feeling. Then he sighed. "Well, that's not entirely unexpected."

"*What?*"

"Mads, I—I suspected someone murdered Elsie Kingsolver," her father said reluctantly. "When it

47

comes to the *San Telmo*, well, a lot of very shady people have been after it at one time or another."

"Including you?"

"I . . . walked into that, didn't I?" Maddison's father sighed. "But yeah, I know a lot about the *San Telmo*. Stuff's been adding up and I *did* notice that the office was ransacked the day before the Kingsolvers cleared it out—I'm the one who bugged the local police into re-opening the case. Hit-and-run," he added, mostly to himself. "*Right,* sure. With her job?"

"Why did you . . . care?" Maddison asked, even though *care* wasn't quite the right word. But there was something here her father was dancing around and it was related to the question of *why* Kevin McRae would go to such great lengths to avenge the murder of someone he didn't know.

"Oh sweetheart, I couldn't just—if you know something is wrong, and you don't help stop it, you're no better than the person doing whatever it is."

"That's not something everyone actually believes," Maddison pointed out.

"No," her dad admitted. "But I couldn't just stand by and let this go."

And that, Maddison thought, staring at her father's face and not caring that she was making him uncomfortable, *is true, even if it isn't the truth, the whole truth, and nothing but the truth.*

"But as for Chris . . . " her father added, trailing off significantly.

"I just can't stand the fact that he and Carrie lied to me," Maddison admitted, and her father put an arm around her.

"It must have been a huge risk, though," he offered. "Letting you in on the same secret that got his aunt killed."

"Yeah, but he still kept the truth from me," Maddison said. Her father winced; that was a sword that cut both Chris and *him.* "And I'm furious that he did, but it's also not really fair to blame him for not immediately taking me into his confidence, is it?" she asked.

"You are allowed to be angry at someone while

acknowledging that they really have done their best by you," her father said with a very slight smile. Again, there were several *levels* to this conversation, and Maddison wasn't sure how many they were currently operating on, and she was actually starting to get an honest-to-goodness headache. And she still didn't know what to do about Chris.

"What am I going to do?" Maddison ended up wailing into her dad's shirt.

"Well, easing up on the sad and conflicted endings might be a start," her dad suggested, patting her on the back. "Watch something happy. And then maybe talk to your friends? Last time you talked with Chris did you tell him what was wrong or just run out on him?"

"Uh," Maddison said sheepishly.

"Be as angry as you want," her dad said gently, "but don't kill a friendship over this. And can I just take this moment to remind you that the search for the *San Telmo* is a dangerous one, and to *be careful?*"

CHAPTER THREE

SAINT ERASMUS'S CATHOLIC CHURCH IN ARCHER'S Grove was a cream-colored jumble of a building; it was a strange combination of stucco and stained glass and had been added to on three different occasions with slightly different colors of paint and a variety of shingling. The half-tended flower beds outside the front doors and the bees attending to those flowers gave it a cheerful, buzzing appearance, at least to two teenagers casing the building one Friday afternoon.

"The oldest part," Carrie said to Chris as they strolled around the church, up the block, across the street, and then back past the church on the other side in the hope of being inconspicuous about casing the building, "is the church itself." She was consulting the church's website on Chris's phone. "They added the current rectory in the eighties and the parish hall in January of 2000—ooh, that's supposed to have stirred up the ghost—"

Chris winced.

"Sorry," Carrie said. Maddison was still not really talking to them, even though Chris had sent her a text letting her know they were exploring the church today. Figuring out when to visit a functioning Catholic church was tricky, especially when your general game plan was to sneak in, find an old parish register and read it for clues, and then sneak out before anyone noticed you. Chris and Carrie were banking on the lack of scheduled events on the church's online calendar and the logical hope that the priest didn't actually spend a lot of time in the church itself. Chris would have felt much more at ease if Maddison had come along, despite having known her only a week or so, but unfortunately she wasn't returning any of his calls.

And he had realized after the fact that the apology he'd sent her might only have made things worse. Carrie must never know.

"It's fine," Chris said, even though it really wasn't. "What do you think *we're* looking for?"

"The attic, or the basement, or the locked filing cabinets?" Carrie suggested. "I actually have no idea. Everything I know about this place I got off its website, and there *wasn't* a link to 'secret treasure maps' on the visitor page."

"That's rude."

"Yeah, *so* inconsiderate," Carrie agreed, and hopped up off the park bench they'd been sitting on. "Come on, it's hot out here and I'll bet the church has air-conditioning."

It took them a minute to cross the street since the traffic light had to cycle back around, and during that moment Chris himself cycled through a series of second thoughts and remembered a few things and ended up frozen in front of the doors.

"Are we sure this is a good idea?"

"No," Carrie said, halfway up the steps. "It was yours, remember?"

But that wasn't the worst part; the worst part was something Chris had just realized. "Carrie, I know where I heard the name of this church before." Carrie paused with her hand on the door handle and rolled her eyes.

"*Now* what's the problem?" she demanded.

"Cesar Francisco," Chris replied, and Carrie opened her mouth to say something irritated but then the name registered and she froze. Then she turned around, slowly, and looked up at the suddenly menacing front of Saint Erasmus.

"*This* is the church he was supposed to have died in? It looks—"

"Really normal," Chris offered. Cesar Francisco had been a Cuban revolutionary in the 1950s, one who had already been approaching folk-hero levels of popularity before his mysterious death and disappearance. All anyone knew was that he had been smuggled onto a small passenger plane bound for the United States and that the plane had never made it to its scheduled destination at a small airfield in Archer's Grove. But Francisco had been a political hot potato; devoted to the rights of the poor and downtrodden. Above all else he had been a thorn in the side of both American and Cuban officials. He might have been a popular hero but he was a political horror.

Of the six different tales of his death, by far the most popular was the one that maintained that Cesar Francisco had, in fact, made it to Archer's Grove, where a waiting CIA agent diverted the plane, killed the pilot, and attempted to kill Francisco, managing instead to wound the man before losing him in a torrential downpour near the old Catholic church. Which had been haunted ever since by the desperate Francisco, searching forever for the sanctuary denied to him when the nearly deaf priest failed to hear him pounding on the doors.

That the body had never been discovered only gave rise to a rumor that the revolutionary had managed to hole up in some forgotten corner of the church—the basement was a popular suggestion—before dying. Other ghost stories suggested that the parish priest had been in on the whole plot and that *his* murder of Francisco was the cause of all the weird ghostly activity. In fact, whichever way you sliced it, Saint Erasmus was haunted by a very vengeful Cesar Francisco.

But that *didn't* change the fact that Chris and Carrie had to go inside, when the church was deserted, if they wanted to get anywhere in their search. And anyway, people had church services in the building all Sunday, so there was no way Saint Erasmus was as haunted as the stories said. Right?

"Shhhh," Carrie said unnecessarily as they eased the church's double doors closed. They entered a narrow corridor decorated with a well-papered bulletin board and a large statue of Mary, and then moved into the church proper. Carrie pushed the doors to the latter open carefully. If they had been in a movie, the doors would have groaned, but instead they gave nothing more than a very small squeak.

It wouldn't have mattered if they *had* dragged the door open on squealing hinges, anyway, because the church was completely empty. And compared to the hot, bright street outside, it felt cool, and it had that echoing hush that tended to settle over buildings with a lot of history and where people were often serious and solemn. It was also dark; the emergency exit sign and the jewel-toned glow of the sunlight filtering through the stained-glass windows were the only sources of light.

After prowling around the whole church looking for possible papers, Chris and Carrie found nothing historical enough to be the church record. It did occur to Chris that there might be a church library or a parish office or something similar—he knew from the website there was a parish recreation hall, where the rummage sale would be held in early August—but the door to that side of the church *was* locked. And for a Catholic church that had existed in the area since 1720, Saint Erasmus was depressingly modern.

"Huh," Chris said, sitting down in a pew and flipping experimentally through one of the books in the rack in front of him. "Even the hymnals were published this year."

"Does this look like Jonah and the whale to you?" Carrie asked. She'd been studying the six large stained-glass windows, each with a detailed scene depicted in jewel-toned colors, and was now paused by the one farthest from the door they'd entered through. On the window a green and blue sea creature with lovingly depicted rows of teeth was frozen in the act of swallowing a tiny figure of a person. It was not the strangest of the windows; there were two depicting catastrophic shipwrecks (one showed a snake gleefully biting someone while a Roman centurion looked on amid the wreckage of a ship; the other showed Jesus walking on water towards a ship still in the process of sinking), and another that looked like a literal depiction of the phrase "I will make you fishers of men."

"Oh, wow. Why does the whale have scales?" Chris wondered, wandering over. It was not only the most disturbing depiction of a whale Chris had ever seen, it was also in the darkest corner of the building, and now that he was in that corner he could see—

"Hey, there's a door over here," Chris said. It was hiding behind a statue of a monk holding a book on which he was balancing the baby Jesus. The door was painted the same color as the surrounding walls, but the knob turned when Chris tried it and the door grudgingly opened. Unlike the front door, this one *did* groan a little, and then it opened into a cluttered storage room full of books, vases, statues, Christmas garland, and—

"C-c-camel!" Chris gasped. Carrie, right behind him, stifled what was either a scream or a laugh or more likely both. The camel did nothing, as it was a plastic camel decorated with red ribbon and jingle bells, clearly intended to be part of a Christmas pageant. It was still terrifying when it loomed up out of the gloom right inside the doorway.

"Christmas camel," Carrie said slightly hoarsely. "This looks more promising."

"This looks like the start of a horror movie," Chris said, heart still pounding. And Carrie didn't get to comment—she was behind him and so had avoided the worst of the camel menace.

"No, seriously," Carrie said. "This looks like a room full of old stuff, if you can get past the camel we might be able to find something."

"He has dead eyes," Chris muttered, but he pushed past the nightmare camel and into the room anyway. It was darker in here, with the only light coming from the exit sign over the door and one frosted window, and it was kind of dusty, but Chris and Carrie set to rummaging with a vengeance. And, of course, with the knowledge that they probably weren't supposed to be back in the storage room.

Despite containing a vast and unorganized stash of Christmas decorations, stacks of old sheet music, tons of dusty devotional books, and a green three-ring binder with "Saint Vincent de Paul Society minutes, do not lose" scribbled across the front in black marker, the storage room refused to give up the ancient parish registers. Chris was just about to give up, tell Carrie there was obviously nothing here for them to find, and suggest leaving when he knocked a box of round plastic Christmas ornaments off the top of a pile of other boxes. They went rolling everywhere, and he had to chase half of the balls under an overloaded clothes rack holding several sad-looking sweaters and all the Christmas pageant robes. Which led to the discovery of yet another door.

This one was so sloppily painted the same off-white as the wall that it must have been actually painted over at some point, and it had a hook-and-eye latch holding it closed. It also had a laminated sign taped to it that said "Authorized Personnel Only" in bright but faded red letters, but this didn't stop Chris from hissing at Carrie to come over to see.

Carrie fought her way through the clothes rack and then sighed. "We aren't authorized," she pointed out. "And you just made me come look at a door you found hidden behind a bunch of coats, there had better not be a land of eternal winter in there."

"They're capes and robes, not fur coats," Chris protested, settling the Christmas ornaments in their box. "And I think it might be the *side* storage room," he admitted, unhooking the door and pushing it open.

The room was certainly half finished, whatever its initial purpose had been. There was one steep step down into a cramped rectangular room with a low ceiling, a dirt floor, and a single dim yellow light bulb, which flickered grudgingly on when Carrie found a light switch just inside the door. But more importantly, as far as Chris was concerned, were the four sturdy metal chests—the better term might be footlocker, Chris wasn't sure—lining the far walls. They had closed lids, but two of those lids had scraps of paper poking out, and that looked promising.

"This might be the oldest part of the church," he said to Carrie as he picked his way down the step. She followed dubiously.

"The stucco does look cruder," Carrie admitted,

fumbling in her shoulder bag and finally pulling out a flashlight—if it had been dim in the previous room it was nearly impossible to see in this one, even with the light on—and making Chris realize that he'd forgotten his own flashlight. "But we might be pushing the whole 'open doors for all God's people' thing a bit far right now."

"I'm just going to look," Chris said, carefully easing the lid of the chest closest to the door open and discovering a mess of crumbling newspaper wrapped around teacups. That was disappointing, but when he moved on to another chest along the right side of the wall Chris unearthed a leather-bound collection of the works of Charles Dickens—a very *old* leather-bound collection of Dickens, probably the oldest thing he'd found yet, even if it was in terrible condition, and suddenly they were—maybe, hopefully—getting warmer. Carrie even looked interested when Chris held up one of the volumes. Even though the chest he was poking through didn't have anything that looked like a parish register, the one up against the far wall had a padlock, although it wasn't locked. Maybe there was something valuable inside it?

"I mean," Carrie continued, following Chris and gesturing with her flashlight so the beam of light went everywhere, "that even beyond the 'we shouldn't be in here' issue, we've now hit the 'we can't convincingly explain why we're in here' issue, and should—"

But what it was Carrie thought they should do (most likely turn around and go back home, after putting everything back the way they'd found it) was drowned out in the horrible sound of old, rotted wood giving way. The floor, as it turned out, was *not* simple packed dirt, but packed dirt over old and rotted wooden boards that covered the old church cistern. It had survived this long only because nobody had walked across it in years—until Chris, on his way to the trunk, just had. Chris had tried to walk over a patch of floor already weakened by heat, humidity, and bugs. A *large* patch of floor, the individual boards of which buckled inward and dumped Chris, Carrie, and a shower of dirt and splintered wood seven feet down into what they later learned was an old, dry basin for collecting and storing water.

Then, as if to put a cap on the entire disaster, the lone and ancient lightbulb swaying in the center of the room flickered twice and went out.

✗ ✗ ✗

It took Chris an agonizing handful of seconds to catch his breath and realize that nothing was injured beyond some painful bruising. Luckily, he'd landed on his side and not on any kind of debris. The cistern was square rather than the more sensible circle, relatively large, and filled with rubble, which Chris discovered when he staggered to his feet, tripped over a what felt like a chunk of brick and mortar, and landed on something soft and squishy which turned out to be Carrie.

"Ow!"

"Sorry," Chris said, scooting backwards on his rear. There was the sound of shifting debris—probably broken bits of the floor that had come down with them—and then Carrie hissing. That . . . wasn't a good sign. Carrie usually hissed because she was angry, in pain, or pretending to be a snake for the school play and trying out method acting. The last play she'd been in had been the disaster-laden, student-written adaptation of *Rikki-Tikki-Tavi* in seventh grade, in which she had played the snake Nagaina. Afterwards, she swore a blood oath, with Chris witnessing, that she would never again be in a theatrical production. Which meant that she was now either angry or in pain, neither of which were good.

"You okay?" Chris asked, and there was an ominous pause. "Carrie?" he tried again, now flat-out worried, "are you okay?"

"For a given value of okay," Carrie said finally, voice tight. "I think I twisted my ankle when I fell."

"Twisted?" Chris asked. He carefully reached out, wishing his eyes would hurry up and adjust to the darkness, and found his cousin's foot. She didn't twitch away so he decided he'd got the uninjured one and tried to give a reassuring squeeze.

"I don't *think* it's hurting badly enough for it to be broken," Carrie said, after some shifting that was probably her testing the ankle's range of movement. "But I'm also not sure if I can stand on it, much less climb out of a pit in the dark."

"Well, can you try if I help you stand?" Chris asked, deciding not to point out that he thought the pit was technically a cistern. He took Carrie's long, wordless sigh as an affirmative, or at least not as a definite no, and got to his own feet very carefully.

The results were not encouraging. Chris managed not to trip over any more debris but it was a near thing, and when he managed to pull Carrie to her feet she wobbled alarmingly and couldn't put any weight on her foot. Chris had to help her settle back on the floor in a more comfortable—well, less awkward position. To make matters even worse the cistern they'd fallen into was made of smooth, fitted stone and offered few handholds, and even when Chris's eyes finally started to adjust to the lack of light he couldn't see a good way out. And at some point in the midst of plummeting headfirst into a black pit—Carrie ordered Chris to stop being so dramatic with his descriptions—they'd lost Carrie's flashlight.

"Which serves me right for gesturing with it," Carrie said glumly as Chris shuffled around the area where she'd landed and found nothing but dust and bricks. He found lots of dust and lots and lots of bricks, though, which did give him the start of an idea.

"I think," Chris said, settling himself on the ground next to Carrie, "that if we pile up the debris I might be able to climb out and then pull you out. But I'm a little worried that I'll pull the edges in on top of us when I try. Or actually," he added as another thought struck him, "we could try calling Professor Griffin? He doesn't work on Fridays and he likes us, maybe he wouldn't ask many questions."

Carrie was nothing more than a slightly grayer blob in the blackness, but Chris was absolutely certain she was staring at him in amazement. He was pretty sure she had even forgotten the pain in her ankle she was staring at him in such amazement. "Yes," Carrie said, after a period of intense staring that Chris was unable to see but could really feel, so perhaps she was developing x-ray vision. "Because Professor Griffin regularly finds us at the bottom of wells in churches we don't even belong to. He won't ask *any* questions."

"I think we're actually in a cistern," Chris offered. "If it were a well there'd be water down here."

"Yeah, I know," Carrie sighed. "A cistern is a major part of the ghost story. I just thought there'd be a sign."

"Well, if you want to get technical there *was* that 'authorized personnel only' sign," Chris said guiltily. "But in that case, I want to meet the person authorized to deal with haunted cisterns."

Carrie flicked a pebble at him, so Chris felt safe enough in poking her back, and was therefore startled when she suddenly grabbed his wrist tightly enough to hurt.

"Wha—"

"Shh!" Carrie breathed. "Do you hear that?"

"You have got to be kidding me," Chris sighed, but

quietly. Now that Carrie had pointed it out he could hear it: there were footsteps coming towards them. Footsteps that were trying to be stealthy, if Chris's admittedly limited stealth skills were right, since they were slow and careful but not deliberate, and whoever was creeping about did not know about the creaky floorboard in the middle of the back room.

Chris abruptly remembered that odd warning from Cliff Dodson at the police station. He hadn't even considered the possibility of being followed—and wasn't it possible for someone to get out of jail if they posted bail, or did that not apply in murder cases? And for that matter, what exactly were the police charging Cliff Dodson with, anyway? Detective Hermann hadn't actually said . . . and did the person now creaking around the storage room know Chris and Carrie had gone in and not come out?

They *did* seem to know that there was a hidden room behind the choir robes, if the zip of metal hangers being pushed aside on a metal rack was any indication. Then there was a scuffling step over the doorway—Chris stopped breathing altogether and held as still as possible, Carrie doing the same right next to him, and hoped against hope that whoever it was would give up and go away after a brief glance into the room—and then a step, and another, right up to the edge of the cistern—and then there was an almighty splintering sound and a surprisingly restrained scream, and this time *Chris* had someone land on *him*. He was on edge and whoever had just landed on him was on edge and they spent probably a good two minutes wrestling frantically with each other before Carrie produced her cell phone from somewhere and turned its flashlight on, and then they got a good look at each other.

"You have *got* to be kidding me," Maddison said.

CHAPTER FOUR

MANY PEOPLE HAD HAD FIGHTS WITH MADDISON. Several people had done things that she swore never to forgive them for; she was still pretending a certain cousin did not exist due to his putting bubble-gum in her hair when she was six. Chris Kingsolver was not the first person Maddison had a fight with and he certainly wouldn't be the last, but he *was* the first person to try apologizing by coded text message. Maddison wasn't sure if this made her feel touched or angry, or if this just made Chris weird, but it was nevertheless what Maddison woke up to on the warm

Friday morning that would see her fall into a deep, dark hole.

She was half-asleep and enjoying it when her phone chimed, and chimed, and then chimed again, and finally she was all the way awake and scrambling on her bedside table for the *still-chiming* phone, which, when she managed a look, proved to be blowing up with texts from Chris. She hadn't spoken to him since that day at the park, and she'd been civil but reserved with Carrie at work because she didn't like dragging people into fights that weren't really about them, and despite her dad's unfortunately good advice she hadn't yet even worked up the courage and righteous anger to explain to Chris why she was mad. And now Chris was texting her as if nothing had happened between them. Maddison sat up in bed and stared at the screen of her phone, which, if nothing else, proved that Chris was motivated, because he had sent her nine texts in a row, and they were all gibberish.

LFMSCFNS, said the first one, and then . . .

OOATHROO

ORPEUIOR

KSSRRDNR

IOOACASY

NRRSHYOS

GRRMSSRO

SYYUOORR

OSSSRRYR

"What on earth?" Maddison said out loud to herself, and then frowned. The last letter in each of the texts, when read vertically, spelled the word SORRY and then SORR, which suggested . . .

Chris, Maddison thought, pulling graphing paper and pen out of a drawer and starting to write out the texts in a grid, *no sane person apologizes via code. This doesn't even* count *as an apology.* But once she'd picked out the pattern it was easy to figure out the message, and reading the texts as a whole, vertically (much like a crossword puzzle), Maddison made out LOOKING FOR MAP ST ERASMUS CHURCH FRIDAY NOON with SORRY filling in everywhere Chris had

74

had a spare space. It was both single-minded to the point of ridiculousness and strangely touching, and also what *did* Chris and Carrie expect to find at the church? They weren't even *members* there. And why did Chris think Maddison cared? Maddison did not care. Maddison did not want anything to *do* with Chris and Carrie. Maddison was not at all touched that Chris thought she was smart enough to figure out a code she'd never seen before all on her own. *And Maddison*, Maddison thought glumly to herself, *was referring to herself in the third person.* Maddison was also lying to herself. That, too, was easier in the third person.

Maddison made herself cereal with chocolate milk and ate it while watching three episodes of the world's most horrifically scripted and cheesy and badly researched adventure-exploration reality show in existence, otherwise known as *Treasure Hunters: Adventures with Robin Redd*. The subtitle was a bit misleading, since the hero failed to find Atlantis, the Loch Ness monster, Timbuktu, or anything more thrilling than a runaway donkey. Then Maddison painted her fingernails with the bright orange nail polish she'd gotten for Christmas. She very resolutely refused to even so much as entertain the idea of going over to the church at noon and helping Chris and Carrie look for the map they were trying to find. She was refusing to do so with such a vengeance that at twelve-twenty her mother swiped the potato chips away, turned off the television, and said, "Shoo."

"Mom! I was watching that!" Maddison yelped, turning the television back on.

"No," Maddison's mom said. "You were a million miles away. You *hate* hospital dramas."

On screen, several nurses in scrubs ran past, calling for a doctor, and yelling about . . . ear transplants?

"Sweetheart, you didn't even notice your father walking in, changing the channel, setting it to record, and walking out the front door," her mom said.

"Really?" This *was* Maddison's dad's secret favorite show. Her dad liked hospital dramas, the more painfully inaccurate the better, because, he had explained to Maddison once, they had nothing to do with his line of work. Historical inaccuracies in television programs drove him up the wall, across the ceiling, and out an adjacent window to go scream at pigeons in the park, to use one of Maddison's grandmother's favorite, if perhaps hardest to understand, sayings. This was because her father was a history professor by trade. The number of teaching assistants he had traumatized when they suggested he use a popular but historically inaccurate movie in class was equal only to the number of popular but historically inaccurate movies out there waiting to be suggested to Dr. McRae, and both were surprisingly high. Maddison's mother, in contrast, took great vindictive pleasure in watching anything at all related to art and art history, and critiquing it mercilessly. Maddison fell somewhere between her two parents, when she wasn't feeling mildly embarrassed for the actors, or puzzled as to why any show that devoted six episodes to an ear transplant storyline was still on the air. Which reminded Maddison. "Wait, what was Dad doing home from work on a Friday?"

"He was at the office late last night so he took a

half-day today," her mom said, helping herself to a potato chip. "And then I think called him about something to do with the hit-and-run, because he's gone down to the police station to annoy people." She rolled her eyes, closed up the potato-chip bag, and made shooing motions at Maddison, who reluctantly sat up and moved the pillows, knocking the sheets of graphing paper she'd been glaring at off the couch as she did.

"Oh," her mom said, looking at the sheet she'd picked up. "Nice transposition. Are you getting into cyphers now?"

"Transposition?" Maddison asked.

"This is a basic example of a transposition cypher," her mom explained, thoughtful and a bit distant, as though she were using skills that had been dormant for years. "You take the message you need to send and rearrange the letters so someone intercepting the message can't read it."

"Huh," Maddison said, wondering how her mom happened to know that.

"An interest in cyphers would mostly involve paper and lemon juice," her mom continued hopefully, "and you wouldn't spend so much time wandering around in the dark in abandoned buildings of dubious structural stability!"

Maryanne McRae had never believed in ghosts and was always distantly worried that Maddison was going to get into physical danger while looking for them. But Maddison had very recent experience that suggested that an interest in cyphers was just as dangerous as an interest in ghosts—Maddison hadn't been in any danger looking for ghosts until she'd added Chris, Carrie, and a cypher to the mix—and anyway, why did her mom know this much about cyphers? Did everyone, and Maddison was just the odd person out? If Chris didn't have such an interest in cyphers Maddison doubted any of this would have happened, but she couldn't entirely blame him for it and what ended up coming out of her mouth was simply, "I *hate* cyphers, they're *confusing.*"

From the sympathetic look her mom gave her as she

folded the sheet of graphing paper in half and handed it back, Maddison knew they were not just talking about cyphers.

"Well, sitting on the couch feeling miserable isn't helping you any," her mom declared. "So, go, get—go deal with whatever has you so wound up," she ordered, shaking out the throw pillows and fluffing the blanket that went over the back of the couch, scattering potato-chip crumbs everywhere. "Read for a while. Take a walk, it's a nice sunny day—go finally have that fight with the boy your father's so worried about."

"Mom, I'm not—"

"Sweetie, you're trying to avoid *something.*"

Maddison groaned, but her mother had always been both perceptive and even more stubborn than her father, so Maddison gave in with just enough bad grace to soothe her wounded pride. She stomped off to her room, threw on a pair of jeans and sensible shoes, and after a moment of hesitation grabbed her fanny pack as well, because she was in a foul enough mood that she didn't care if she got caught in a church with an EMF meter and a headlamp. And if she stayed in a foul mood all the way to Saint Erasmus, she wouldn't have to think about the fact that she was going to go visit the church.

The church was just barely within walking distance of Maddison's house, and Maddison walked that distance with a purpose, which left her sweaty and out of breath and hardly less grumpy than when she started. Jogging, Maddison thought to herself, stopping with both hands on the iron stair rail and taking deep breaths of flower-scented air, was going to have to go back in her morning routine. Being this was out of breath was embarrassing.

It also didn't do much to improve her black mood. So it was probably a good thing that Maddison didn't meet Chris and Carrie when she stomped up the front steps of the church. She'd have bitten someone's head off. Then actually getting inside the cool and dimly lit interior of the church had the not-entirely-welcome effect of calming Maddison down.

The McRaes were vaguely Catholic. Maddison's maternal grandparents were regular weekly churchgoers, so habit took over and Maddison sat down in a pew to take a few deep breaths and mentally send a prayer heavenward, because that was what you *did* in church.

Our Father who art in heaven, she thought, *give me patience. Or the strength to forgive? If that will help? I have no idea who I'm angrier at, Dad or Chris. Actually, I might not even be angry at either of them, but if that's the case then I* am *angry that I'm not angry that I wasn't asked if I wanted to get mixed up in this whole mess. But then, it's not that I don't want to be involved. I do. I just wish I'd known what it was I was getting into before I got into it. I'm in this up to the neck anyway—in fact, I think I'm in something up to the neck anyway because of* Dad, *so it's a little insulting that they think keeping parts of the truth in the dark will make me safer than telling me everything and letting me help.*

. . . oh. Well then.

Suddenly, Maddison wished she'd been less irritated and had caught up with Chris and Carrie at the church at noon. If she wanted to be involved in the search for the *San Telmo,* then stubbornly extracting herself from further fact-finding missions was not useful, and anyway, where on earth could Chris and Carrie *be*? The church wasn't that big.

It was at this point that Maddison, who had been sitting in a pew at about the middle of the church, almost jumped out of her skin at the sound of an almighty crash.

She stood up, uncertain, trying to pinpoint the source of the violent but muted noise. The problem with being raised vaguely Catholic, of course, was that Maddison thought that poking her nose into the church basement was rude in a way that Chris and Carrie didn't. Also, because she knew what the interior of a Catholic church was supposed to look like it had not occurred to her to go looking for doors that were supposed to be locked.

And anyway, Maddison thought as she edged through the half-open door behind the statue of Saint Anthony, she'd never actually been inside this particular Catholic church, let alone with all the lights out, most churches didn't store their Christmas pageant stuff in a room directly off the main church, and *hello*, that was a scary camel.

Maddison carefully turned the camel around so it was not *looking* at her, and wandered farther into the room. There were an impressive number of old hymnals stacked on the tables, a statue of Saint Francis that someone was halfway through repainting, and . . . behind the rack of costumes she thought she heard whispering. Remembering every single one of the legends about Saint Erasmus being haunted, Maddison swallowed both her fear and her common sense and edged around the coat rack. And found a door marked "Authorized Personnel Only"—which Maddison was not—with a hook-and-eye latch that was hanging suspiciously open.

This is a terrible idea, Maddison told herself as she

pushed the door open, *a terrible, terrible idea.* It opened into a pitch black room that smelled faintly of long-undisturbed dust. But at least, Maddison thought, the latch was hanging open, which *decreased* the chances of this being a ghost she was chasing since ghosts were fond of walking right through doors without unlocking them.

The voices, if there ever had been voices, had ceased altogether by the time Maddison landed harder than she'd intended to on a step that was steeper than she'd thought, but this was not actually Maddison's worst moment of carelessly rushing in. Her worst moment of carelessly rushing in was when she began walking farther into the room *while* digging her head lamp out of her fanny pack, instead of sensibly waiting to get a light before she went farther into the room. Her attention was focused half on digging around in her fanny pack and half on watching where she was going, but then, ghosts were generally not solid and a live person wouldn't be able to see her unless they were wearing night-vision goggles.

Shoot, and she'd left her pair at home, locked in a drawer because they were technically her mom's and even more expensive than the EMF meter.

So, of course, Maddison managed only three steps before her foot landed on air instead of solid ground, and she toppled forward and *down.* Somebody screamed, and it was most likely her, but Maddison was far too busy trying to fend off whatever she'd landed on, which was *alive,* and *moving,* and all the while also trying to get her breath back after landing hard—on something *alive and moving*—and it was only when the until-now-unnoticed third person off to her left turned a light on that Maddison got a good look at who she was trying desperately to fend off.

"You have *got* to be kidding me," Maddison said.

Carrie at least had the grace to look sheepish. Chris just looked delighted to see her, until he apparently realized where they were and that the last time they'd spoken Maddison had stormed out on him, at which point he made a valiant attempt to look distressed instead. It didn't work.

CHAPTER FIVE

"Okay," Maddison said when glaring furiously at Chris got boring. Plus, it was hard to glare at someone when you were both mostly in the dark. "I have to admit this is a new one." She stood up, the better to fold her arms and look irritated, and tried to smack some of the dust out of her jeans. The dust in her mouth, bitter and gritty, was bad enough. "When you said you were going to a church to look for clues I thought you meant the stained glass windows had clues in them or something, not that you were planning to *fall down a well*."

"Falling down a well wasn't part of my plan," Chris said.

"Then what was?" Maddison asked. Chris hesitated, and it didn't actually matter if he was stopping because he'd gotten a spider in his eye and needed to blink it out, Maddison had had *enough*.

"Don't," she said, and she knew her voice came out nasty and she didn't care. "If you can't tell me the truth, the whole truth, and the truth as you know it when you found it, I don't want to *hear* it. I am *sick*," she continued, and kicked a brick into the opposite wall, hard, "of being kept in the dark for my own protection"—she used violent air quotes on that last word, even though they could barely *see* them in the light from one measly phone flashlight—"when I have been dealing with this for *longer* than you have!"

There was a ringing silence, and then Chris said, "Longer?" in a small voice. Maddison discovered that it was *hard* to explain a secret you only half understood yourself.

"I know my dad is hiding something," she finally

said, and was glad it was dark so she didn't have to see Chris's face in detail. "I know it has something to do with the *San Telmo*. I don't know what, he won't tell me, he's *never* told me, but he's been hiding it for a very long time. And I can deal with that, because he's my dad, and I've trusted him my whole life, but it still—still scares me." Great, now she was crying; she was going to get dust in her eyes. "So I can't handle another person pulling the same thing." Maddison swallowed, cleared her throat, and added, "And the whole 'it's for your own protection' thing won't work, we're the same age and I'm stuck in this stupid well just the same as you."

Then she tried to wipe tears off using the underside of her shirt, and there was a *thwack* and a yelp from the general vicinity of Chris and Carrie.

"Ow!" Chris said, which meant Carrie was the one thwacking people. "Maddison, I'm sorry. We—I—we don't know much more than I already told you," he admitted, "but, well, your dad was kind of . . . scaring . . . us."

"The whole I'm-going-to-take-this-archivist-job-really-quickly-even-though-I-already-refused-it-three-times thing was scaring you?" Maddison asked, slowly lowering herself to the ground where she'd been standing. "Imagine that. It was certainly scaring *me*."

Ow, brick chips. Not fun to sit on.

"And he kind of turned up at Aunt Elsie's office when I was cleaning it out and wouldn't leave me alone," Chris added. "He was polite and helpful and everything!" he hurried to add. "It was just too much right after Aunt Elsie died and I was all paranoid about—everything. Somebody had ransacked the office before I got there, too."

"Dad mentioned that," Maddison said, startled.

"*Really?*" Chris asked.

"Yeah, in passing."

"That's new," Chris said. He sounded bewildered. The whole conversation was strangely unreal, especially since Maddison was sitting in the bottom of a well in the dark and couldn't see Chris or Carrie.

"What Chris is dancing around saying," Carrie cut

in, trying to be calm and logical and missing only by a hair, "is that neither one of us wanted to admit to someone we'd only just met and who we both really liked that we were slightly suspicious of her dad. And yes, I asked you to come to the Archive with us because you were Dr. McRae's kid—because I didn't want to talk to your dad and you were actually approachable and not, like, staring creepily at Chris."

"Oh," Maddison said.

"Also I lost the necklace on purpose because we had all Aunt Elsie's stuff packed and we still hadn't found the floorboard we were looking for." Carrie actually sounded guilty.

"But then someone came in and stole it from the office," Chris added. "I know, because it was in Sketchy Guy's bag when he broke into our house. I stole it back."

"Did you leave it in a desk drawer?" Maddison asked, not even bothering to ask who Sketchy Guy was because this conversation had gone so far past bizarre she didn't even care anymore. "Because my dad *did* say there was a necklace in a desk drawer, and when I asked him if he recognized it he said he just turned it in to the lost and found."

"Yes, but I called the reception desk and they said there *wasn't* a necklace in the lost and found," Carrie explained.

"Oh-*kayyy*," Maddison said. "That's weird. Anything *else* you feel like telling me?"

"Carrie probably sprained her ankle," Chris volunteered. "And she *had* a flashlight but she dropped it when we fell." Which was why they were all squinting at each other in the light of Carrie's cell phone.

"Also," Carrie said, "unless one of you has freakishly good phone reception we *can't* call Professor Griffin for help. There's no reception down here. Or at least I have no reception," she added as an afterthought.

Chris groaned and checked just as Maddison did, but they all had the same service provider, which apparently did not offer enough coverage for using your phone at the bottom of a pit for anything other than eerie lighting.

"Well. It's a *well*, we fell down it, and if I can ever tell anyone about this I'll never hear the end of it," Chris moaned. "Can you imagine all the Lassie jokes?"

"In a frightening turn of events," Carrie said, "I actually agree with something you said previously, Chris. This is a *cistern*."

"It's the old one, from before the church had running water or was, you know, part of a neighborhood," Maddison explained, patting the ground around where she was sitting for her headlamp. Everything else had survived the fall into the we—cistern, but she'd dug the stupid thing out of her fanny pack right before she'd fallen in and been holding it when she fell. She had probably dropped it. And she *liked* that headlamp.

"It's supposed to be where the ghost comes from," Carrie added. Her voice wobbled only a little bit.

"Exactly how much research into this church did you do?" Chris asked. He had gotten back to his feet and was groping for the wall.

"Just what was online about the ghost of Cesar Francisco," Maddison answered.

93

At exactly the same time Carrie said, "A lot, because I couldn't figure out what we were supposed to be looking for?" Maddison felt a brief flare of glee at not being the only person who researched ghosts anymore. "We're looking for a parish register, we think," Carrie said to Maddison, as her cousin tripped over something in the background and called the floor an unkind name and they all tried very hard not to think about the ghost. There were a lot of variations to the basic story, since the mysterious disappearance of Cesar Francisco, along with the story of the screaming caves, were Archer's Grove's two most popular legends. In some versions, Cesar Francisco had fallen into the cistern in the church's courtyard as he was taking his last breath, and the fact that the cistern had been both dredged and drained since then—with no body turning up—had done nothing to stop the rumors that the church was most haunted in the area around the cistern. Where they all were right now. In the dark.

"What's in the parish register?" Maddison asked. "And . . . what is Chris doing?"

"I'm trying to see how big this cistern is," Chris said, as Carrie shined her light in his general direction, revealing Chris, a surprisingly sturdy-looking stone wall, and a scattered pile of masonry. He waved. "Why is it so full of bricks and stuff, anyway?" he added, giving one an experimental kick.

"Because . . ." Carrie leaned back against the wall, thinking. Maddison decided against running into a wandering Chris in the dark or standing up to trip over more bricks, and scooted over to sit next to Carrie. "When they stopped using the cistern they boarded it over so nobody would fall in," Carrie explained, "and then somebody built an outbuilding over it, and then they extended the church which just sort of absorbed it, and I guess it's just been sitting here crumbling into pieces for years waiting for people dumb enough to fall through."

"Like you did?" Maddison asked.

"Well, like *Chris* did," Carrie said, and then they both winced as Chris tripped over another stone. The floor was a tangled mess of ancient brick dust and crumbling bricks, with some scraps of old cloth and a sprinkling of splintered wood, making it difficult to stay balanced walking across the floor, let alone climb out. And to make matters more difficult the boards across the cistern had not all fallen into disrepair. There were still some crisscrossing the cistern, and in the light of a single cell phone Maddison and Carrie could even see places where someone had long ago put down particle board to cover places where the original boards had fallen through.

"We aren't the first people to fall in," Maddison said. "Or, well, this isn't the first time the boards have fallen in."

"How can you tell?" Chris asked, pushing hopefully at the largest fallen board.

"Particle board," Carrie said. "Also, they had a serious dispute over keeping the old cistern or filling it in when they got indoor plumbing in the early forties."

"You did a *lot* of research on this church," Maddison commented.

"You should see her actual school reports," Chris

suggested. "They're scary. And detailed. And once, when we were in eighth grade, her teacher told her she didn't need an annotated bibliography and she cried."

"I . . . did," Carrie admitted. "I was afraid I'd get thrown in jail if I plagiarized. And I never got into the habit of throwing things together last minute," she added, presumably for Chris's benefit.

"So, research?" Maddison asked.

"Yes!" Carrie said. "Research. Lots and lots of research, because I had no idea what I was looking for—we *think* we need a parish register from 1725 written by the priest who witnessed the fleet going down—and I had no idea how to find it."

"Which . . . is why you were in that storage room?" Maddison asked.

"The original Spanish mission that was out on the coast somewhere eventually merged with another parish and all their stuff moved here," Carrie explained. "So if anything from 1725 survived it should be here."

"Do we even know the church still *has* its old parish registers?" Maddison asked.

"Aunt Elsie found *something*," Chris said simply. "And this was the last thing she was looking at."

It was pretty hard to argue with *that*. "I think I might have an Ace bandage in my bag," Maddison said instead, "if someone else knows how to wrap a twisted ankle." She paused and thought her offer over. "Or if you do that when you twist an ankle. Do you wrap a twisted ankle?"

"You do," Carrie said. "I think. Why do you have an Ace bandage if you don't know how to wrap one?"

"Mom gave it to me in case of emergencies," Maddison explained, upending her EMF meter, several pens, a packet of tissues, a bottle of aspirin she offered to Carrie, her tape recorder, and a crumpled Band-Aid into her lap before finding the Ace bandage crushed at the very bottom. "She doesn't like me wandering around in the dark tripping over things, says she had a brother who stepped in a hole in the woods and couldn't walk out and wasn't found for days."

"Yikes," Carrie said, trying to flatten the Ace bandage.

"Which is funny, because I have three uncles and she's never told me which uncle it was."

"I would have thought the wandering around in the dark looking for ghosts would worry her more," Carrie said.

"Oh, she doesn't believe in ghosts," Maddison explained. Which would be nice, right about now, what with the deep shadows in the corners of the cistern and the feeling Maddison had of invisible eyes staring at her.

"Speaking of ghosts," Chris said suddenly, maybe because he could feel the atmosphere, too.

"*No,*" Carrie said almost over the top of him.

"But Carrie, it's like a giant elephant in the room," Chris protested. He was halfway across the cistern, still feeling his way around the edge and stumbling over dusty bricks.

"You are *not* getting worked up over the ghost of Cesar Francisco," Carrie said. She shifted a little and bumped her newly wrapped ankle. "*Wow,* that hurts. There's been weird legends attached to this church since the thirties—the guy who made the stained-glass windows went crazy from the lead fumes and tried to swim to heaven, there's a plaque on the Leviathan Window—and people are supposed to have heard and seen strange figures in the water of the cistern after Cesar Francisco disappeared," she went on, despite having just told Chris not to get worked up over the ghost. "But it's only been in the past decade or so that the weird stuff has happened. After the cistern was drained—actually after the first couple of boards fell in—some local kids told the police they saw glowing mist and evil red eyes down in the cistern."

"Oh, that's never good," Maddison commented. She wasn't sure telling ghost stories was a great idea, but Carrie was likely in more pain than she was letting on and anything that distracted her was a good idea. Also, anything that distracted Maddison was a good idea too, because Maddison was slowly realizing that she had neglected to follow one of her dad's longest-standing rules. Maddison wasn't supposed to leave the house without telling someone where she would be going and how long she planned to be gone. She'd *never* forgotten that particular rule before, and her dad was going to be both angry and disappointed. But more importantly, Maddison was starting to suspect her dad had a concrete *reason* for that rule, a reason related to treasure hunting and whatever was endangering archivists, and that he was also going to be worried.

"Right?" Carrie asked, and Maddison dragged her focus back to Carrie and the haunted cistern. "It got worse, too. There were spooky noises at night, there were eerie lights coming from the room where the old cistern had been—at that time the church hall hadn't been built, so that storage room with the camel?"

Everyone shuddered at the mention of the camel.

"That storage room was the church library and they had Bible study in there, so there were people in and out of that room all the time," Carrie finished. "There are loads of possible ghost sightings, and they still see stuff. Sometimes people walk by and get a whiff of rotting flesh, there are cold spots, and if you take a picture next to the door to the storage room you're more than likely to see orbs."

"And you waited until we got here to tell me this stuff?" Chris demanded.

"I didn't expect you to find the old cistern, which has *actually* been supernaturally quiet since the early two thousands, or drag us all down into it while looking for clues!" Carrie was getting close to yelling.

"Guys," Maddison said, trying to interrupt. She was very proud of how even her voice was even though she had just discovered something startling and a bit scary.

"What am I supposed to do if we meet a ghost?" Chris asked, sounding genuinely irritable and tripping over yet another pile of rubble. He kicked it, scattering bricks everywhere, and yelped in pain.

"Whatever you were planning to do when you met the priest whose church we broke into!" Carrie suggested, also sounding irritable and pained and not at all noticing the strange electronic humming that had just started up. Well, started up at about the point Maddison had tried to interrupt—clearly she wasn't the only person feeling irritable today. And Maddison was perfectly ready to sit through a blowup, if Chris and Carrie needed one. But now was maybe not the best time?

"Guys!" Maddison finally said, under her breath but as loud as she could make it. The hairs on the back of her neck were standing on end. "Look!"

When they snapped their attention back to her, Chris looking sheepish and Carrie mortified, Maddison held out her hand, EMF meter in a death grip. It was humming away merrily, and the red indicator light was showing both their faces in eerie red.

"It's probably just because of somebody's cellphone," Maddison said uncertainly as Chris switched to a worried expression and Carrie went directly to horrified. "And who knows what kind of Frankenstein wiring this thing could be detecting. But maybe we could just . . . " she said.

"Sit over here in a corner and huddle?" Carrie suggested, because her cousin hadn't waited for a suggestion before bolting from the opposite corner to her side, and was already doing it.

"Okay, sure, let's go with that," Maddison agreed, inching closer. The EMF meter continued humming and she was irrationally glad her back was to the wall. It was one thing to go looking for ghosts, it was quite another to have your EMF meter behave in a way that was only supposed to happen in horror movies. Maddison had never had this happen before.

"Has anyone ever even seen a ghost with spectral form around here?" Maddison asked. As suddenly as it had started, her EMF meter stopped squealing.

"Cesar Francisco," Carrie said into the silence. "Dozens of times. Do you think it *was* the wiring?" she added, with a nod to the device now lying quietly in Maddison's lap.

"No idea," Maddison said. "Is there wiring in here?"

"There has to be some," Chris offered, "because there was a lightbulb on its last legs in here. It died right after we fell in the cistern," he explained when Maddison poked him and waved in the direction of the surrounding blackness. "I wouldn't be surprised if there's more, and in terrible shape. As far as false positives go," he said, "it's a safe bet."

"Uh-huh," Maddison said, instead of what she really wanted to say, which was "this is the most interesting thing my EMF meter has ever done, and I am both scared and terrifically excited."

Chapter Six

IT WAS NOT POSSIBLE TO SIT IN AN AWKWARD HUDDLE in the dark of an empty cistern waiting for a ghost to appear for very long. Chris lasted fifteen minutes after the EMF meter stopped squealing before his nerves got the better of him and he started fidgeting. Carrie lasted fifteen-and-a-half minutes, at which point Chris bumped her injured ankle and she shoved him halfway across the cistern, and Maddison discreetly backed out of the altercation while they were flicking random bits of debris at each other. They didn't actually notice that her silent preoccupation was foreboding until she finally spoke up.

"So, um, when we checked our phones for reception did you guys happen to check how much battery you had left?" Maddison interrupted when Carrie had to stop to get brick dust out of her hair.

"No," Chris said, trying to remember when he'd last charged his phone. It had been recently, maybe.

"Yeah, I was at something like eighty percent," Carrie said.

"And I was at seventy," Maddison said. "I'm at six percent right now."

"Wait, what?" Chris asked, and pulled his own phone out of his pocket to discover that he was running on three percent battery. This, he thought to himself, was unusual even if he had forgotten to charge his phone overnight again.

"Aren't malfunctioning cell phones supposed to be a sign of paranormal activity?" Chris asked.

"Oh, I was hoping you wouldn't know that," Maddison said. "I'm kind of impressed that you do. I could explain away the EMF meter going haywire but this is starting to look less like a coincidence and more like a genuine haunting."

Chris did not admit to how much research he had done into aliens and ghost hunting while worrying about Maddison storming out on him. Especially since it had probably been equal to the amount of research Carrie had done into the church.

"The phones might just have run down the battery searching for a signal," Carrie suggested, not looking terribly convinced herself. Her own phone, since she charged it every night, was still at ten percent, and after a brief argument she left hers on and Chris and Maddison turned theirs off.

"So that we have some sort of backup," Maddison said. "Although I hope we don't need it."

"And not that I don't enjoy being stuck in a well with the both of you," Carrie said, "but we really do need to figure a way out of here, preferably without getting arrested for trespassing." She was holding her phone on her lap, and looked appropriately grim and glowing in the blue-white light. The same light was making Maddison look ethereal, which was just not fair. Chris sighed.

"I still think our best bet is going to be making a pile of junk and climbing up it," he admitted. "This cistern isn't very big, and from what I can tell it's *full* of junk."

"Yeah, did you find anything interesting when you examined every inch of this space in the dark?" Carrie asked with a hint of cheerfulness.

"No," Chris admitted. "Not even the remains of Cesar Francisco."

"Don't joke about that," Maddison said darkly, joining Chris and giving the pile of bricks he was standing next to a poke.

"This looks like a good place to start piling bricks," Chris offered.

"Yeah, actually," Maddison said, and started kicking more bricks over. "Just try not to annoy"—she dropped her voice—"anything."

Chris paused with an armful of lumber and a dubious look for Maddison. "Tell me you don't feel

109

like we're being watched," Maddison demanded in a whisper. "That EMF meter didn't go off by mistake, and I *don't* think the temperature is what's giving me goosebumps!"

"I don't really think there's a ghost or even a skeleton in here," Chris said. "There aren't even any closets!" It was a terrible joke and it fell flat; he could feel Carrie giving him an unimpressed stare from all the way across the room.

"Yeah, I know, that was terrible," Chris admitted. "But you don't have to kill me with your eyes, or whatever you're doing with that death glare. I can feel it from all the way over here, you know."

"Uh, Chris?" Carrie said.

"Yeah?" Chris was now wrestling an armful of dusty wood into a stack and Maddison was shifting the debris already against that wall into a more solid pile, so they both had their backs to the wall they'd left Carrie sitting against.

"I'm . . . over here?" Carrie said, from *directly beside him,* and Chris stifled a scream. If she was right next to him, and Maddison was right next to him, then who had just been giving Chris a death glare? "I found Maddison's headlamp," Carrie continued while awkwardly angling herself so her back wasn't facing the other side of the cistern. Chris couldn't blame her. His heart was pounding, *and* it felt like it was stuck in his throat. "But, uh, that was about a second *before* I started limping towards you, and I haven't been glaring?"

Wordlessly the three of them turned cell phone flashlights on the far end of the cistern, revealing absolutely nothing in the cistern except Chris, Carrie, Maddison, and a lot of old bricks.

"Clearly it was just the wind," Chris said weakly.

"Staring at you?" Maddison whispered.

"Well, sometimes we personify the elements," Chris protested, not sure where he was going with this comment and wishing the hair on his arms would stop standing up in fright. "So it stands to reason."

But what it stood to reason he never had to invent, because right at that moment a light but unmistakable breeze picked up and everyone froze. It came from the opposite side of the cistern, *where they had just been sitting*, and it carried with it the faint smell of dust and dirt and death.

"Okay, not a personification of nature," Carrie whispered, backing up against the wall as the air on the opposite side of the cistern grew brighter and brighter and settled into a human figure and Maddison gave a strangled squeak and then said, "They're real," in a choked voice.

Chris was frozen in shock, but Carrie had an iron grip on his elbow and must have had a similar one on Maddison's, because she was able to drag all three of them backwards despite being the only one injured. Then something rolled under her feet and her legs went out from under her, and the fact that she'd only had one good foot to start with, combined with her death grip on Maddison and Chris, dragged them both over right along with Carrie when she fell. Maddison yelped, Chris tried to but nothing came out, and the now-glowing figure got more and more distinct, and closer and closer to them, reaching out one hand like it was trying to touch them or point at them or—or something, Chris wasn't sure at the time, terror chasing every other thought from his mind. Later, he would think he heard, very distantly, a sick and horrified sort of moan from Carrie, but he was never sure if it was his imagination filling in the gaps. All he knew at the time was that the ghostly figure repeated its reaching action, more insistently but no more comprehensibly, all the while glowing and wavering brighter and brighter. The strange dank smell got stronger and Chris felt his ears pop—and suddenly a brilliant electric light flared on and the ghost was gone.

"Good heavens, that's an awful smell," said a completely unfamiliar voice directly above him, and Chris craned his neck backwards to see a pair of glasses attached to an angular but still-young face, and—oh no.

The face was attached to a clerical collar.

CHAPTER
SEVEN

THERE WERE WORSE THINGS THAN BEING CAUGHT in an "Authorized Personnel Only" part of a church you didn't attend by the priest of the church after you had broken through the floor of the side storage room. Being discovered in an "Authorized Personnel Only" part of a church you didn't attend by the priest of the church *and* the eternally nosey father of your friend and awkward crush, for example, was worse. Having it happen after you had just had a soul-bearing conversation about suspecting him of complicity in the tragedy that befell your aunt went beyond description. Dr. McRae just seemed to have an uncanny ability to turn up *everywhere,* in this case in the side storage room of the local Catholic church, with the local Catholic priest and the largest high-powered flashlight Chris had ever seen.

It only made things worse that the first thing out of Dr. McRae's mouth was, "Mads, did you fall down a *well?*" His tone of voice was exasperated but fond as he braced himself on the edge of the cistern and grabbed Maddison's outstretched arms without needing instruction. Chris had never known that Maddison's dad called her an adorable shortened version of her name; it made the man far too human. Dr. McRae pulled Maddison up and out of the cistern with apparent ease, although he must have hauled a little too hard because he pulled her over on top of him and they fell down in a heap.

"Ow," Dr. McRae said, muffled. "That was ill thought out."

He was acting eerily like Professor Griffin, Chris thought, and this was not at all fair.

"Carrie's ankle is twisted," Maddison said as she got

shakily to her feet, and then there was concern on Dr. McRae's face, and he and the priest, who introduced himself as Father Michaels and was far more young and energetic than Chris had expected, bustled over to the edge of the cistern and started trying to pull Carrie up without injuring her further. Or at least they would have if Carrie, dead white and with a look of absolute horror on her face, hadn't refused to move.

"One of you needs to go call the police," she said instead, and when Chris gave a strangled squeak she gave him a look of anguish and explained. "When I fell I put my hand down on—on a hand." She swallowed. "And I have a horrible feeling the round thing I can feel under my back is really a skull."

"Yup," the woman with a tight gray bun and "Coroner" on her jacket said, letting Detective Hermann pull her out of the cistern and peeling her gloves off. "It's a body." Detective Hermann, who'd arrived in record time, sighed and produced a roll of caution tape, stopping Father Michaels in the middle of a slightly rambling account of who had been in the church's back rooms in the past year.

Chris was inclined to think that the body—the very old and mostly desiccated dead body that they had been sharing a cistern with for over an hour before Carrie discovered it—was Cesar Francisco. It only made sense, as they'd found it in the church's old cistern and it was not a fresh corpse. Father Michaels, however, seemed sadly resigned to the idea that the body could be anyone's.

He'd been the one to help Chris pull Carrie out of the cistern while Dr. McRae and Maddison called the police—which meant that Chris didn't have any idea what Dr. McRae had told the police about what they'd found, so that was another thing to worry about—and then he'd dug an ancient and lopsided folding chair out of the junk in the back room so Carrie didn't have to stand on her twisted ankle, and when the police had arrived he'd explained how few people ever went in the church's back rooms and exactly who they were with enough detail and precision that Detective Hermann looked impressed. "The camel scares a lot of people away," Father Michaels admitted. "I use these rooms for storage—my grandmother's dishes, in fact. It's too dark and the floor isn't very sturdy, but my grandma left me two whole trunks of good china dishes when she passed and I haven't got any room for them in the rectory, and ceramic dishes aren't going to be hurt by a little dark and dust, so they've been living back here," he said. "My grandfather's copies of Dickens shouldn't be out here," he added. "But he used to write dirty limericks about the characters in the margins and when I had the set in the rectory every time I turned around someone was flipping through them and getting scandalized."

Detective Hermann squinted at the priest, but all he offered was, "Then the good thing is that we won't be inconveniencing the parish if we have to cordon this area off for the crime scene investigators."

"Oh no, that shouldn't be a problem," Father

Michaels said. He gestured absently with the binder labeled "Saint Vincent de Paul notes, do not lose" Chris had noticed earlier. "Most people wouldn't go into either of these rooms for longer than they absolutely had to even if you *paid* them. I think the youth group traditionally sneaks down here every year in the middle of the night when they have their spiritual retreat in the church hall, but they do it when the chaperones are asleep so I've never found a way to bring it up to Mrs. Woodley without giving her a nervous breakdown, and it's so hard to find a good religious instructor that I can't risk it; this will just give me a reason to keep them out. Now, if you don't mind," he added, "I've got a young woman with a sprained ankle and I'd like to take her out of the damp basement and maybe wrap it . . . "

Detective Hermann looked at Carrie, who'd been shivering since she'd found the body, then at Maddison—who had been very quiet since seeing the ghost, then at the coroner in the process of stringing up caution tape, and said, "Of course." Chris was left with no choice but to help his cousin up and follow the priest. What he really wanted to do was stay by the cistern; he didn't like the idea of leaving the body in the hands of a bunch of police officers he didn't know. He had the maybe-not-so-irrational fear that it would disappear if he did, in the same way he had a maybe-not-so-irrational fear that someone had paraded Cliff Dodson in front of him the other day in a purposeful attempt to scare him.

✗ ✗ ✗

"So," Father Michaels said to three distinctly bedraggled kids and an also bedraggled Dr. McRae once they were clustered awkwardly in the middle aisle of the church, clasping his hands. "I have one question, and it's very important: would anyone like some of the monkey bread I made this morning?"

This offer resulted in nothing but stares. Father Michaels frowned. "Maybe some tea? I might even have some soda still in the fridge. And then we can discuss what you three were doing back here in the first place?"

"Oh," Chris said, guilty.

"Tea sounds fine," Maddison said weakly, and Carrie nodded.

The rectory, which turned out to be through one of the doors up by the altar that Chris hadn't noticed, was exactly the kind of place Chris would have loved to explore if he hadn't been stomping on that urge hard out of guilt. It was a small and very vertical house, with a long, spindly staircase and a bunch of smallish rooms with high ceilings, an ancient sea green refrigerator in the tiny kitchen and mismatched lace doilies on the mismatched living room furniture. Father Michaels put the binder in the exact center of his dining room table with the solemnity he would give to a Bible, and then put a tea kettle on to boil and microwaved a plate of monkey bread while everyone stood in an awkward cluster in the kitchen. Then he herded everyone back through the dining room and into the living room, explaining as he did that, "We've been looking for that binder for *months,* it's at the center of a massive argument about the Christmas poinsettias."

The living room seemed even smaller than it actually was, since Father Michaels had stuffed it with books, stained-glass pieces, and dinged-up musical instruments to such a point that it was difficult to sit down without knocking anything over.

"Oh," Father Michaels said absently when Chris almost backed into a cymbal stand, "don't mind those, I play a bit."

A bit was possibly an understatement, considering the trumpet behind the couch, the electric keyboard balanced on a folding chair, and the triangle laid carelessly on a sofa cushion, but Chris restrained himself to just looking and sat down on his fingers. It was agony. The priest had an apothecary's chest against one wall and a bookshelf full of geodes against another, and it was the sort of room you could explore for a day and not notice half of the contents, provided you weren't feeling extraordinarily guilty and nervous or limping badly.

"The good thing," Dr. McRae said, gently rewrapping the Ace bandage around Carrie's ankle, "is that this is nothing more than a mild sprain. You could be walking in a couple of days, as long as you don't do anything to redamage it."

"You're sure?" Maddison asked, and her father pretended to look offended.

"Mads," he said, spreading his hands in a harmless "Who, me?" gesture. "You can trust me, I'm a doctor."

"Of the *arts,*" Maddison pointed out, arms crossed.

"Well, true," Dr. McRae said. "But I have all sorts of certifications and I do know my basic first aid, so you are going to be fine," he told Carrie. "Provided you don't fall down any more wells."

"I'll admit that I wasn't looking forward to working on my Sunday sermon all evening," Father Michaels said when he'd successfully settled a tray of mugs on the coffee table and passed around plates of cinnamon-sugar bread. "But I wasn't really looking to replace that with a fun evening of dealing with the haunted cistern."

123

Chris tried desperately not to fidget. To his surprise, Dr. McRae, who was sitting right next to Father Michaels, *did* fidget.

"And it *is* partly my fault for leaving a hole like that covered with flimsy boards that can't hold the weight of a teenager without breaking," Father Michaels continued with a sigh. "Would you be kind enough to tell me why you were there? At least so I can put up better warning signs?"

You could have heard a pin drop or a cricket chirp. Or the *mrrrt* of the gray long-haired cat who squeezed out from under the armchair Father Michaels was sitting in. The cat glared at everyone with bright yellow eyes, took a swipe at Father Michaels that he dodged with a skill that clearly came from practice, and climbed up the tablecloth draped over a side table. The cat settled directly next to Dr. McRae's plate.

"*You* don't get to comment. Where were you when this was going on?" Father Michaels said to the cat.

"Staring at me through the window," Dr. McRae volunteered, eying the cat nervously and sniffling.

"Because I spent a good five minutes sitting on the rectory steps worrying before Father Michaels got back from the hospital and could let me in, so, Maddison?"

"Uh," Maddison said, putting her mug down hurriedly. The mugs all had a grinning cartoon image of Jesus on them, and according to Father Michaels had been sold by the youth group to raise money for the Mary Garden.

"They weren't very popular," the priest had admitted while pouring tea. "I think it was the fact that the eyes seem to follow you around the room, or maybe the strange greenish cast to Our Lord and Savior's skin."

He had, as a consequence, bought almost the entire stock for his own use, despite having decent china teacups from his grandmother stored in the side storage room. Chris was beginning to think there was something evil in that room, and that it got into and warped everything.

Maddison was still staring into space, obviously trying to come up with a reason for falling in the cistern. She was failing, and Chris decided that the awkward silence had gone on long enough.

"It's a school project!" he blurted out, and got pinned with horrified looks from Carrie and Maddison, although Carrie's was more of a *you-have-got-to-be-kidding-me* horrified look. Dr. McRae gave him an oddly amused look.

Belatedly, Chris remembered that Carrie had only recently told him that "it's a school project" wouldn't work in this case.

"I mean, not a school project, *exactly,*" he amended, and the murder in Carrie's eyes went down to assault and battery. "But we did a section on local early Florida history at the end of the school year and some of it was really interesting and w-we were looking into it a little more." There, that could actually work. And it was based in the truth; they *had* done a section on local history, in late April. "And we were . . . trying to find out more about this early Spanish mission that disappeared and the priest who recorded it, and it was supposed to have been part of this church. So we were, well, looking for some of the old parish registers to see if they mentioned him."

That sounded studious enough, and if Carrie and Maddison backed him up they might even get Father Michaels to *help* them find the parish registers. They would at least have a reason to ask him.

"You were looking into the *Santa Maria* mission?" Father Michaels asked.

"Yes?" Carrie offered. Maddison was involved in some sort of staring contest with her father that she appeared to be winning.

"Well, that's a new one," Father Michaels said, getting to his feet and shifting the cat, who growled at him. Chris was just frantically trying to think of better excuses to use when Father Michaels went on and stopped him short. "Normally I only ever get graduate students in history programs asking about the mission," he said, and removed the statue of Mary and the tablecloth from the side table the cat had been perched on, revealing that the side table was actually a freestanding safe.

"The thing about grad students," Father Michaels added as he spun the lock open, "is that they've spent enough time doing research that they call me first, and only end up wandering around the church falling down stairs and into the holy water fount or sitting on rosebushes and putting their feet through the ceiling by mistake on the third or fourth visit."

He swung the door of the safe open. "Technically," he added, "the mission was named *Santa Maria, Estrella de la Mar*, in honor of"—his voice took on the sing-song quality of someone reciting—"*Santa Maria, Nuestra Dama, Estrella de la Mar.*"

"Saint Mary, our lady, star of the sea," Dr. McRae said, breaking off his staring contest with Maddison. "One of the titles of the Virgin, patroness of sailors?"

The cat took an experimental swipe at Dr. McRae, who resumed his resigned glare but transferred it from Maddison to the cat. Then he sneezed. Father Michaels, meanwhile, shifted papers around in the safe for a bit and then came out with a crisp, blue-gray box, utterly unexpected in a church rectory but incredibly familiar to Chris. Next to him, Carrie gave a tiny gasp, so she had recognized it too.

The obvious explanation hit Chris only now, when it was too late to do any good. *Duh. If you have a fragile, possibly damaged, historically interesting seventeenth-century parish register then you don't actually hide it away like the lost treasure in some summer blockbuster. You take precautions against theft and against damage from the elements.*

In short, you keep it in an acid-free box in a safe where the priest can keep an eye on it.

CHAPTER EIGHT

To add to Chris's complete and utter feeling of mortification, when Father Michaels put the box down on the coffee table to unfold it and take the book out, the box proved to have a stamp on the lid marking it as the property of Edgewater Archives. This was less a coincidence than it was another moment of *Duh, Chris, what else were you expecting?* because the supplies you needed to preserve books in an archive weren't cheap, especially for organizations that needed only a few things. Acid-free paper and boxes and stuff like stainless-steel paper clips were expensive and hard to buy in small quantities, and so the Edgewater Archive bought extra supplies with their bulk orders and sold them to local institutions for pennies. It was the community outreach program Aunt Elsie had been the most protective of. She would have donated things at no cost and in fact sometimes did, except then people took what they didn't need or never used it. Still, the Edgewater Archives stamp on the box was painful to look at.

"We only have two or three of the old parish registers," Father Michaels said. "This is the only one we have that mentions Father Dominic Gonzalez. He didn't start keeping a parish register until 1722, when there were enough church members to make it worthwhile," Father Michaels continued, paging delicately through the brittle paper. "And it isn't very much information, so you might be disappointed."

"What does it say?" Carrie asked.

"On this day of our Lord the fifteenth of September, 1729, were offered masses for these souls," Father Michaels read haltingly. "Uh, my Latin isn't the greatest," he added, "but it goes on to name the men—Juan Calasanz, Antonio Arnau, Paul Sanchez, Gregorio Sanchez, Juan Simon Rodriguez—'who were among many others lost in the terror of the deluge that sank the fleet of our majesty's galleons in the year of our Lord 1717. Father Gonzales offered many prayers that we be spared ever more such a deluge and a wreckage, which he had seen with his own eyes from the threshold of this, our mission. May we face adversity with fortitude and trust in God's will, Amen.'"

"Amen," Maddison echoed, and then blushed. Father Michaels grinned. Then he put the parish register back in the box and passed it to Carrie, who was sitting closest to him, the clear intent being to let them pass the book around so everyone could look at it.

For something Chris had faced down a ghost to find, the parish register was surprisingly plain. It was a slim book bound in leather, with crumbling pages of intricate cursive in ink that had faded to a pale brown. The entries, although Chris could pick out the occasional name and a few words that he could guess, were all written in Latin and impossible to decipher. He flipped a few pages and then handed the register and its box carefully to Maddison.

"But that's really all there is about Santa Maria, Estrella de la mar," Father Michaels explained, "and about Father Gonzalez. Now there are *other* great sources of information about the early history of this church and the Catholic community in this area, some of them even in English, but if you want more first-hand stuff about Father Gonzalez you'd have to hike out to the ruins of the Mission and poke through the wreckage."

"Because they left records at the old Mission church?" Carrie asked. Father Michaels nodded.

"Some of the more determined graduate students I've talked to actually went out and poked around the old Santa Maria mission, because we *know* from other sources that the priest who packed up that mission left a lot of stuff out there," Father Michaels said. "But . . ."

"But it's dangerous?" Chris offered.

The priest seemed to argue with himself for a

second. "That course of action isn't . . . one I'd rec-
ommend," he said finally. "Not very many people who
go looking for that mission manage to find it, and it
scares a lot of the ones who do."

"The mission scares them?" Maddison asked.

"Wait," Carrie asked almost over the top of
Maddison's question. "How hard is it it to find this
mission?"

"That part of the Florida wilderness is supposed
to be haunted," Father Michaels said sheepishly. "At
least according to the six or so people who have come
by to take pictures of the window for their paper and
ended up giving me a blow-by-blow account of their
accidental re-creation of a found-footage horror movie,
complete with shaky camera footage and a lot of mis-
cellaneous twigs bent into sinister shapes."

"Oh," said Maddison, perking up without seeming
to realize it. "Really? What kind of haunted is it?"

Dr. McRae closed his eyes in resigned mortification.

"General Florida weirdness?" Father Michaels
offered, packing the parish register back into its box.

"The mission is in ruins now, and it isn't marked on most maps of the park, but if you ask any of the rangers they can tell you which trail gets you close and what to look out for. It's not as though it's some secret lost temple or anything, I don't know why people insist on thinking it's haunted. I honestly think it isn't anything but active imaginations and too many scary movies, since every single person has told me about something different happening to them, but I live next door to a ghost so I hardly have room to talk."

"The ghost we *just* had a run-in with," Maddison added, and Carrie mumbled, "Not supposed to talk about that sort of thing," under her breath.

"Oh, probably," Father Michaels sighed. He had, Chris remembered, been very careful not to turn his back to the cistern and tried to get them all out of there as fast as possible, and he had been more resigned than surprised to find a skeleton in the cistern. Maybe he did believe in the ghost.

"Have *you* seen a ghost in the cistern?" Chris

couldn't help but ask. He got another shrug and hand wiggle in response.

"I've heard weird noises," Father Michaels explained. "Strange smells, too, but that could just be small mammals getting in the church and then dying, and Grey here . . . " He poked the cat, who attempted to bite him and then hopped off the couch to rub happily against Dr. McRae's feet. "He *hates* that part of the church. Not that Grey doesn't hate most things," he added, "and he's not even supposed to get into that part of the church after the incident with Mrs. Kennedy and the lit advent wreath—but there are also a couple of people in the parish who can't even go in that side storage room at all, either because of the consequences or that camel, I'm not sure."

There was a moment of silence as everyone shuddered at the thought of the camel.

"All that being said," Father Michaels continued, "I've never actually seen a ghost, even when I went in there and blessed the place—but then I missed the skeleton, so make of that what you will—and I think there's an overflow pipe buried under all the junk down there that sometimes lets the wind in. If there *is* anything in that cistern I don't think it's actively evil, or I'd have taken more drastic measures before now." He grinned. "And you three are without a doubt the strangest thing I've ever found back there."

With that he more or less let the whole matter of them getting caught where they weren't supposed to be drop, and instead asked Chris, Carrie, and Maddison a number of questions about the research they'd been doing into Father Gonzales and the history of the church. Luckily Carrie really had done her research and Chris had skimmed the church's website so they didn't seem too obviously to be faking it.

"Yeah, Father Gonzalez is a bit of a local legend," Father Michaels explained when Carrie asked if he was the brown-robed figure in the center of the church's rose window. Which was another puzzle to Chris, because that window was blue, so shouldn't it have been "the blue window"? "They used to say he carved a mission church out of rock and sheer determination, and he did so much for the sailors on this island that even the other congregations liked him. Mad George Lucian is supposed to have come up with the window designs for this church after he saw Father Gonzales in his dreams for seven nights in a row, standing in front of a different stained-glass window every night." Father Michaels sighed. "But that story sounds too neat and tidy to be true," he added. "It's sad, because the reason Father Gonzales was such a friend of sailors is the 1717 Fleet disaster. A truer legend that a lot of people skip over is that he saw the whole thing and it devastated him. He spent—well, you heard that entry in the parish register—he spent the rest of his life praying for the souls of those who were lost in the wreck, and the priest who succeeded him followed his example. It's why the name of this church has changed but the saint has always been a patron of sailors."

"Saint Erasmus is a patron saint of sailors?" Carrie asked.

Chris looked at her in surprise. *Saint Mary, our lady, star of the sea,* Chris thought, *isn't it pretty obvious?*

"Yes," Father Michaels said, "one of the major ones. He gets shortened to Saint Elmo sometimes, and San Telmo."

Chris very nearly jumped in surprise. Maddison looked intrigued again.

"And before anyone asks, no, I haven't ever had a run-in with ball lightning while I've been priest here," Father Michaels added. He'd apparently figured out what Maddison's area of interest was because he addressed the comment mostly to her. "Or Saint Elmo's fire." He looked fondly at the irritable gray mop that was curled comfortably on Dr. McRae's feet. "Though he likes to poke me in the nose in the middle of the night and when he builds up enough static electricity he zaps me, but that doesn't count."

"Saint Elmo's fire is this weird bluish static electricity that builds up on ships," Maddison explained to Carrie and Chris in an undertone. "It's also called ball lightning, and it's sometimes thought to be supernatural."

"Like a green flash?" Chris asked.

"I don't know if a green flash is considered supernatural," Maddison said thoughtfully. "That's when the sun suddenly looks green when it's setting, right?"

"Yeah. But I've never seen it," Chris said.

"Professor Griffin has once, remember?" Carrie reminded him. "Two years ago? He was so excited we got him a cake."

"*Or,* it could have a perfectly reasonable explanation, like the refraction of light," Father Michaels said, bringing the side conversation to a halt.

"Like the disappearance of Cesar Francisco?" Maddison asked. "You didn't expect the body in the cistern to be him," she added when the priest frowned.

"I've never been entirely convinced he died there," Father Michaels admitted. "There are some holes in the legend; for one thing, my predecessor's predecessor was never that deaf." He shrugged. "But then again, I've never seen the ghost, so I can't say he is or isn't Cesar Francisco."

"He didn't look like anyone in particular," Maddison offered, but Father Michaels was frowning at his cat, who was now genuinely snoring on Dr. McRae's feet. Dr. McRae had been making increasingly strange faces over the course of the conversation, and his eyes, Chris now noticed, were red and watering.

"I realize I should have asked this earlier," Father Michaels said. "Are you by any chance allergic to cats?"

Dr. McRae tried to offer a polite denial but he was interrupted halfway by a violent sneezing fit, and Maddison and Father Michaels jointly decided that it was time for everyone to head home before, as Maddison put it, "Dad starts having trouble breathing."

"Can I talk to you for a second, Father?" Dr. McRae asked as they gathered up a pile of mugs and dislodged Grey, who slunk under the armchair and hissed at the world. "In private," he added, and sneezed again. Father Michaels looked puzzled but agreed, and Maddison must have picked up on something because she grabbed Carrie and made a beeline for the body of the church and then down the aisle and into the entryway. Carrie gave Chris a significant look and he hurried to follow them, so the only spying he managed was a glimpse of Dr. McRae and Father Michaels bending over the rack of prayer candles. Then Maddison was pushing the second set of church doors shut and studying the bulletin board.

"I saw some prayer cards I want to look at somewhere on here," she announced, and Chris and Carrie spent a confusing five minutes reading about pancake breakfasts on the bulletin board while trying not to wonder what Dr. McRae and Father Michaels were talking about. There wasn't really room for all three of them in the tiny hallway, either, and eventually Carrie sat down on a set of steps that turned out to lead up to the choir loft and Chris found a visitors' log. He thought about signing it, but then the memory of Sketchy Guy stalking them loomed up in his consciousness, and he flipped through it instead. It was a big, heavy book of good-quality paper, and it went back years. Some of the signatures in the book had been there since the late eighties. Early in the nineties Chris's absent page flipping hit a snag and he was fingering the ripped edge when Carrie came up behind him.

"Find anything interesting in there?" she asked him. Maddison was frowning in thought with two different prayer cards in each hand and another tucked under her chin.

"There's a page missing," Chris said, but just then Dr. McRae and Father Michaels came through the doors and he let the matter, and the cover of the book, drop.

Whatever Father Michaels and Dr. McRae had been talking about they didn't feel inclined to share, because Dr. McRae went right for the doors outside while fishing a Kleenex out of his pocket, sneezing. Father Michaels paused just inside the doorway to the church.

"I'll keep you in my prayers," he said to Chris, Carrie, and Maddison. "If that's all right with you. And remember that the doors of this church are always open to you." He paused. Then grinned ever so slightly. "Except maybe not the ones marked 'Authorized Personnel Only.'"

CHAPTER NINE

DETECTIVE HERMANN WATCHED THE BODY BAG GET wheeled out to an ambulance with a deep scowl on his face. "We'll need statements from all of you at some point," he said when the group neared him. "But for now"—his gaze fell on Carrie's wrapped ankle and the way she was leaning heavily on Chris—"it's fine if you just go home. Just don't leave on vacation or anything without contacting us first."

Chris felt such a statement was moderately ominous. He was unexpectedly grateful for Carrie's injury; he was pretty sure it was the main reason everyone was cutting them so much slack. Even so, Chris wasn't looking forward to explaining what he'd been doing at the church to a police officer. Especially since he was a little—okay, kind of a lot—worried that there were people in the police department working against them. They still didn't know if Dodson had been the only one behind Aunt Elsie's murder . . .

The trip home was tense.

It wasn't entirely Dr. McRae's fault, either. Maddison's father offered to drive them all home in a tone of voice that suggested he might run someone over if they didn't accept. *Maybe that's more suspicious than helpful,* Chris thought to himself, *but he really does look like he wants to murder someone.* Then he drove the few miles from Saint Erasmus to the street the Kingsolvers lived on in silence broken only by the occasional sneeze. Apparently he was really very allergic to cats.

The only good thing was that Maddison had called

shotgun as soon as they got to the parking lot, and so Chris did not have to sit next to Dr. McRae and try to make polite conversation, because all he could think of—*So, you're really allergic to cats* and *By the way, I'm still seventy-percent sure you tried to kill me*—were conversational openings hand designed to get him glared at. At the least. Who knew what a sneezing, itching, already irritated Dr. McRae would do if bothered?

In the end, it was Dr. McRae himself who broke the silence, by turning to Maddison and asking, in a tone low enough that Chris and Carrie could pretend not to hear, "Do we need to have a talk about the 'telling someone' rule?"

"Can we pretend I realized that I forgot the rule when I was halfway down a cistern in the dark?" Maddison asked, sinking low in her seat despite wearing a seat belt. "Because that's totally what happened, and I think falling down a cistern in the dark and then getting stuck there for hours is punishment enough for forgetting—oooohh, Mom is going to be—I don't even *know!*"

"Horrified? Smug? Tempted to never let you out of the house ever again?"

"Yeah," Maddison said. "So, I'm already very sorry and you don't need to lecture me. Because I already lectured myself for an hour."

"Okay," Maddison's father said-sneezed. "That's fair. It's not getting you out of trouble—and I *am* telling your mom what happened—but it is fair. Your mom says you were in a foul mood when you left?" he added.

"Yeah," Maddison said in a small voice.

"Did you hammer it out or do I need to beat somebody up?"

There was a slight possibility, Chris thought, that if he threw himself from the moving car he'd survive the impact and subsequent fall into—he checked outside—a crocodile-infested canal. It might be preferable to sitting the conversation through to its logical conclusion.

"Dad!" Maddison yelped.

"Well, do I?"

"*No!*" Maddison said firmly.

"Please no," Carrie added, not helping at all. "I'm too used to him."

"Ah, well," Kevin McRae said. "It had to happen someday. Oh—and at least it wasn't that Tyler fellow who used to follow you around making idiotic comments about your eyebrows."

"*Daaaaaaaad!*"

"Although he *was* on the football team," Dr. McRae pointed out.

"What's the 'tell someone' rule?" Chris asked, now even more afraid of the direction the conversation was going. Carrie, the traitor, was giggling hysterically into her fist and would probably start encouraging them when she caught her breath.

"It's simple, really," Dr. McRae said, sobering. "Maddison has to tell someone where she's going and how long she's going to be gone whenever she goes out. Everyone in the family does."

"I forgot to do it this afternoon," Maddison admitted. "I was angry when I left for the church and it completely slipped my mind—how did you know where I was, anyway?"

"Luckily for me, when you're angry you also stop being 'tidy Maddison' and turn into 'leaves everything in a pile on the floor' Maddison," Dr. McRae said. "I got back from the police department needing to tell you something and you weren't there, but you'd left me a decent transposition cypher with the translated message written in underneath telling me that you were going to the church at noon and that you were sorry. Very sorry, judging by the number of times the word was repeated."

"I didn't mean to make you worry," Maddison offered.

"Normally it wouldn't be a problem," Dr. McRae sighed. "I would have waited for you to get home and given you a lecture when you did, but something happened today that all three of you deserve to know about, and I was . . . worried. Which is why I drove out to the church and pounded on the door for five minutes before I remembered there's nobody in on Fridays."

"Sorry," Maddison said.

"We're lucky Father Michaels is a calm sort of person, and doesn't get upset if you scare his cat," Dr. McRae said.

"Aaand, again, sorry," Maddison said.

"Ah, but I didn't fall down the cistern and sprain anything, so I got the better end of the deal."

Actually, Chris suspected Dr. McRae had gotten the worse end of the deal, because he'd been so worried. But he didn't say anything.

"So, what was the thing we deserve to know?" Carrie asked nervously.

Dr. McRae looked at Maddison and then at Chris and Carrie in the rearview mirror, and pulled abruptly into the parking lot of the local grocery store.

"It won't be in the papers until tomorrow," he said when he'd parked and turned around to face all three of them with only a slight crick in his neck. "So I'd appreciate it if you two don't tell your parents where you found out about this until after the news breaks, because this isn't the sort of thing that should be leaked, but I happen to have a friend on the force who tells me a lot more than he should." He sighed. "Cliff Dodson—the man who admitted to killing Elsie Kingsolver—they found him dead this morning."

"Wait," Maddison said. "Dodson? Like, threatened park rangers and tried to shoot Chris and Carrie, that Dodson?"

"Dead? *How?*" Carrie asked.

Dr. McRae sighed. "Yes, Maddison, *that* Dodson," he said. "And well, I was down at the police department because they wanted to ask me questions about the time he tried to shoot at me and three park rangers . . . " He started to trail off, because Carrie was giving him her best worried look.

"Oh," Maddison interrupted. She looked like she'd just made a connection and she couldn't believe it. "Cliff Dodson was Sketchy Guy, wasn't he?"

"Sketchy Guy?" Dr. McRae mouthed, and then he

shook himself. Carrie was still giving him huge worried and puzzled eyes, and he sighed.

"How did he die?" Carrie asked.

"They're pretty sure it was suicide," he admitted. Chris gaped at him; Carrie was frowning in puzzlement and Maddison looked shocked, and if Dr. McRae had been intending to avoid most of the details because of their tender years he crumbled in the fact of their combined confusion.

"They found . . . they found him hanging," he said grimly. "Not a *lot* else it could be. You don't fake things like that very well in real life." He cleared his throat. "Although anyone trying would have to realize how strange it would look. Out of character, I mean," he clarified. "Dodson had a rap sheet the length of his arm and no sense to go with it. He was not the type to kill himself for getting caught."

"So he really wasn't the type to commit suicide?" Maddison asked quietly.

"He wasn't the type to even come up with the idea," her father told her. "Just—it's probably nothing, I'm probably overreacting because you're growing up and falling in—"

"*Don't* say it!"

"Cisterns," Dr. McRae finished innocently. Maddison actually growled at him. "But I still worry," he continued, serious again. "About *all* of you," he added, although he seemed to direct it especially at Carrie.

Something about Carrie seemed to bother Dr. McRae, not that he was in any way rude to her. In fact, he seemed to be especially careful with her, but that might simply have been because she was injured; he looked at her as though she made him sad for some reason.

"I thought this mess was over," Dr. McRae said, and, wow, he was gripping the steering wheel tightly with that one hand. "I thought the *threat* was over, and now one more person is dead. I can't deal with you going missing, you understand? And if you are going to run around researching the history of the mission you all need to do more careful research before diving in like that," he finished. Chris didn't entirely like the way he said "researching the history of the mission." It sounded far too knowing, and if there was anyone who was going to guess what they were up to and become a gigantic stumbling block it was Dr. McRae.

Well. That was the whole problem still, wasn't it?

"What were you talking to Father Michaels about?" Maddison asked suddenly, and Dr. McRae sneezed in surprise.

"Oh, that? I was, just checking that, well . . . " He looked at them in the rearview mirror and bit his lip. "You know that ominous moment in a movie where the main character goes to ask the librarian about the secret book of arcane spells, or what have you, and is just about to leave with the information he needs when the librarian mentions that it's the oddest thing but they're the second person to come in asking about that book?"

"Yes," Maddison said slowly.

"Oh *no*," Chris said.

"Actually you got lucky this time, the last person

who came in asking about the parish register and Father Gonzalez was a family historian from Idaho."

CHAPTER
TEN

THE PROBLEM, CHRIS ADMITTED TO HIS COUSIN LATE that evening, after convincing two sets of parents that Carrie had tripped coming down the steps of the church they had visited to look at stained-glass windows, was that they hadn't really accomplished anything.

"What do you mean?" Carrie asked, chewing on a pen. She was sitting inside Chris's room this time, mainly because her family had stayed over for dinner and then she and Chris had disappeared to copy out the instructions for their summer reading project. The adults were in the living room, hashing out the pros and cons of getting security systems installed in both houses. Chris actually had lost his summer reading project instructions within about a day of getting them. He felt guilty for losing his copy, and he and Carrie actually had talked over the assignment, for about fifteen minutes, but it didn't take that long to decide that *Billy Budd* was a safer bet than *Moby Dick*, and then they'd turned to the more pressing matter of Aunt Elsie's clues and the final resting place of the *San Telmo*.

"We still don't have an eyewitness account of the sinking of that ship," Chris said, "and I'm pretty sure Maddison told her dad everything she suspected about what we've been doing and is going to fill him in on everything we told her today."

"Yes," Carrie said slowly. "But is that going to be such a bad thing? Because now we don't have to pretend *not* to know about the letter she left us. And Dr. McRae might even be trying to help us—he *did* check who else had been looking for that parish register. Honestly, none of us would have thought to do that."

"I . . . just don't know," Chris said finally. He tried to imagine perfectly harmless reasons for all of Dr. McRae's actions since they'd met, and started to get a headache. "He *does* know a lot about old Spanish mission churches," Chris admitted.

"That's what he did his dissertation on," Carrie said immediately, as though that were a fact any average person would know. "I deal with suspicion by researching people!" she said in defense when Chris stared at her incredulously.

"I guess there are worse ways of dealing with suspicion," he said. Being suspicious on principle was a perfectly good coping method, as far as Chris was concerned, but Carrie just sighed at him in response.

"We might be able to get his help finding the Santa Maria mission if we ask nicely and avoid glaring at him," Carrie pointed out. "So you need to try not to be the most *obviously* suspicious person on the planet next time you see him," she finished.

"Why can't we just ask Professor Griffin?" Chris moaned.

"Because he doesn't know a thing about archeology unless it's under at least a foot of water?" Carrie suggested. Professor Griffin was usually more interested in the geology under the archeology, and he'd admit as much to anyone who listened, which was a constant source of amusement for his students and a point of ongoing despair for his historian and archeology colleagues.

"Okay, true. But he has a boat," Chris said.

"We don't know that Dr. McRae *doesn't* have a boat," Carrie pointed out. "Or that we're even going to *need* a boat. But yeah, I've been wondering if it might be a good idea to tell Professor Griffin what we're up to. I'm just not sure how to bring it up in a way that won't immediately send him to Aunt—our parents."

Chris knew she had been about to say "immediately send him to Aunt Elsie" because that was the person Professor Griffin told if Chris and Carrie were being what he referred to as "bewildering." Chris had been thinking of her too.

"He could still tell the whole thing to Aunt Elsie,"

Chris said. "Except he thinks mediums are a waste of space and that ghosts are figments of our collective unconscious, so there's no way for him to contact the dead. Do you think he'd like Maddison?"

"Well, he tolerates you," Carrie said, and they commenced shooting rubber bands at each other until Carrie's mom poked her head in the room and announced that it was time for people with sprained ankles to hobble out to the car and go home.

Carrie and Maddison went radio silent on Saturday because, Chris discovered over a series of frantic texts from Carrie early Saturday morning, they had been invited to a summer tea by Mrs. Hadler. Chris couldn't imagine Mrs. Hadler doing anything as human as eating, unless she was eating the bones of tardy children and drinking tea made from boiled detention slips. He also couldn't figure out why Carrie sent him twenty angry text messages demanding he tell her where he'd put the lace tablecloth from last Christmas dinner until she sent him a picture of herself wearing it as a shawl, along with her mother's straw sun hat with a plastic lei wrapped around the band, her locket, and a sundress with added lace frills.

It's a costume party? he replied to her text, which was the picture along with a comment that she had found the tablecloth in the baking cupboard.

Apparently, Carrie sent him. Mrs. Hadler called me this morning and told me she'd forgotten to mention that they had a Sunday hat contest and to bring a shawl because the church hall gets cold.

That's . . . nice?

So enthusiastic. I'll see you sometime tomorrow. Btw, my phone is working fine today, yours?

Fully charged, Chris replied, feeling his amusement at Carrie in a flower-covered hat evaporate. The ghost in the cistern was still a mystery.

Luckily, Chris had a day unexpectedly free, since Carrie and Maddison were occupied. And Chris suspected they were plotting something beyond how to sneak out of the party with extra cupcakes.

So he spent half of the day reading about ghostly manifestations on websites of varying quality and pretending he hadn't noticed the online applications to the pet store, movie theater, and plant nursery that kept popping up in his inbox. His mom was relentless, but Chris figured he had about a week to stall or find something he could convince her took up too much time for him to hold a job. Searching for buried treasure would probably do it, but his mom was not likely to believe him, since he'd tried using that excuse before with a much less valid treasure map. So Chris avoided thinking about the job applications, and instead got nowhere in his quest to figure out what had been up with the ghost in the cistern.

He hadn't really talked it over with Carrie or Maddison. Carrie, at least, was probably already well on the way to convincing herself the ghost had been nothing but a trick of the light, and there had been no time to talk to Maddison, but Chris was way more unsettled than he wanted to be.

What they had seen just seconds before Dr. McRae and the priest had found them had been a real ghost.

But it had not been Cesar Francisco. Cesar

Francisco was supposed to appear, when he appeared in ghostly form, as a dark-haired figure in an old-fashioned gray suit spattered with blood. The ghost Chris, Carrie, and Maddison had seen had been wearing a red T-shirt and what were obviously sneakers. After a full hour of researching increasingly dubious websites Chris came to the conclusion that ghosts were not capable of changing their clothes. Either the ghost they had seen was some sort of super ghost, or everybody who had ever seen the ghost of Cesar Francisco had misreported what he had been wearing, or (and much more likely) the ghost they had seen was not Cesar Francisco. And if the ghost was not Cesar Francisco—and since his clothing would seem to date him from *after* Francisco had died that was a pretty good bet—then who was he?

Chris spent twenty minutes searching for instances of ghosts who haunted Saint Erasmus who were not Cesar Francisco and getting nowhere before he ran out of interest and likely sources and started getting a headache.

The headache had worsened and he'd started to

develop a crick in his neck before he finally realized, at about ten thirty, that he was glancing at his window every three seconds and expecting Carrie to come through it, even though she almost never did during daylight hours.

Carrie's busy, Chris told himself firmly, *and you're going to do something useful with your time, so chill.* But the day wore on and he couldn't chill and he couldn't even manage to settle, and finally Chris glanced at his calendar and realized why he was so twitchy.

It was the twenty-fifth. Aunt Elsie's paycheck for the month would have come today, and usually she'd have invited the family over for dinner and a movie. He was missing her again. And he'd been trying to avoid even thinking about her, because it hurt too much, and solving the last puzzle she'd ever left him was just as good as remembering her, right?

It really, really wasn't, and Chris knew that.

So, Chris saved about six tabs on his computer, one of them a job application with one question answered, and had half a sandwich and a glass of water, which helped with the headache. Then he begged the use of the car off his mom, who was sitting at the kitchen table watching square-dancing videos online and taking notes on the competition.

He had to ask her three times she was so involved, and when he finally got the keys and told her where he was going and also why, because there was maybe something to that rule the McRaes had, he went out the door as fast as possible so she couldn't trap him as a captive audience. She was itching to drag someone into a discussion of how talentless her major competitor was. The square-dancing community was a small community, but it was a competitive community.

The local florist was badly understaffed, which made Chris feel guilty for not filling out the application. He poked around the display cases for fifteen minutes, watching three different people buy red roses with guilty expressions and one tiny elderly couple buy each other Venus fly traps before there was a break in the action big enough for him to make it to the counter. Then the girl at the cash register had to go in the back and search for five minutes, but eventually she sold him a small bouquet of asters.

Asters were small, purple, daisy-like flowers also known as Michaelmas daisies, and they had been Aunt Elsie's third-favorite flower, after lilacs and common white clovers. She'd liked that they were purple; it was a less-than-common color for a flower. Asters could also be light purple, which was an even less common color than regular purple. They were the flower that she tended to get as a gift, because clover was not something you got from a florist and people never seemed to remember lilacs except in the spring. Asters had then somehow turned into the one thing everyone got Aunt Elsie whenever she was stressed or worried or running around demanding that some sort of higher power give her strength and patience.

That one meaning of the Michaelmas daisy actually *was* patience Chris had learned only in the past year, but oh, how it fit. And since Chris suspected that if his aunt were up there somewhere watching him she was making a lot of alarmed faces and muttering to herself about common sense and his lack thereof, if Chris was going to bring flowers to his aunt's grave he was going to bring her asters.

He hadn't been to the cemetery since the funeral, which—Chris stopped to think under a statue of an angel, her wings furled and head hanging in her hands, and was almost attacked by a goose—had been only three weeks ago. It felt like forever. Aunt Elsie's grave was still newer than any of the others surrounding it, and simpler since she hadn't wanted any inscription, and it looked barren to someone who had last seen the gravesite buried under funeral flowers.

Chris didn't *really* hold with talking to the tombstone like you were talking to the person you'd lost, but he sat down cross-legged in front of the slab of black granite anyway, laying his small bouquet down before it.

"Hey," he said. "I miss you."

Nothing earth-shattering happened. But Chris sat for a moment, in the warm sunshine with a light, sea-touched breeze rustling the grass, and birds trilling somewhere in the distance, and let himself feel lost and scared and more than a little worried he was going to be murdered for a sunken treasure, and also very glad he'd known his aunt for as long as he had. It didn't hurt nearly as much as he thought it would.

It was only as he got up to leave that he realized the green grass covering Aunt Elsie's final resting place was peppered all over with little white balls of clover, and that what he'd assumed was a tuft of grass up against the gravestone was actually an intricately woven crown of those same clovers, a day or two old and slightly wilted. It was delightful and charming, if maybe a little creepy at the same time.

"I'm not the only one, am I?" he asked his aunt. "We must be driving you *crazy* down here."

169

Chris went one blissful night without anyone climbing in his window before it started up again. But it wasn't just Carrie this time—he was woken up disgustingly early on Sunday to someone tapping on his window, and when he finished his minor heart attack and crawled out from under the covers to look he found Maddison waving at him.

"It's seven in the morning," he whispered when he pushed the glass up. "What are you—Carrie put you up to this, didn't she?"

"Carrie told me this was the best way to wake you up," Maddison said innocently, leaning her elbows on the ledge. She was standing on the garden bench and she didn't even have black circles under her eyes. Everything in life was unfair.

"Did she happen to give you a *reason*?" Chris asked. "Or are you both just trying to scare me to death?"

"Get dressed and come on," Maddison said. "We're going to the park, and I brought muffins."

"Which park?" Chris asked, finding a pair of pants and a shirt and some shoes.

"Those don't match," Maddison pointed out helpfully from the window.

And a *different* pair of shoes. Chris stomped off to the bathroom to dress, feeling like a goldfish in a fishbowl. Carrie was sitting in the backseat of the car eating carrot muffins when Chris hopped out to the driveway, still trying to pull his left shoe on. Dr. McRae was sitting in the driver's seat, also eating muffins and looking faintly puzzled. Chris realized that he was wearing a tie-dyed purple and green shirt with a T-rex on the front, and choked.

"I was under the impression you wanted transportation for a *date*," Dr. McRae said as Chris and Maddison clambered into the car.

"Did I say that?" Maddison asked. "Because I meant that I wanted transportation on a particular date. To the state park. For our *summer research project.*"

Carrie sighed, Chris realized that this was one of those things he was never going to live down, like the lizard incident in third grade, and Dr. McRae made a sound like a strangled duck and began beating his head against the steering wheel.

"So, is this why Carrie was too busy last night to come through my window at eight thirty?" Chris said over the thump of Dr. McRae banging his head against the steering wheel.

"Three hours in the library going over maps and old land records on microfilm," Carrie said happily, proving without a doubt that she was not human. "Why? What incredibly important thing were you afraid I'd interrupt?"

"Uh," Chris admitted. "I read the first three chapters of that book for English class?"

Carrie would have tried checking him for signs of being a pod-person but apparently Dr. McRae had rules about doing that sort of thing in the car.

"I didn't enjoy it or anything," Chris protested. "I just thought 'what would Carrie do if she had an evening free?' and then I did the most boring thing I could think of."

He didn't mention that he had also spent part of

the evening writing and then discarding five different speeches to give to Professor Griffin on the topic of treasure hunting. Dr. McRae was in the car. And if he mentioned that he was practicing a "so we're searching for buried treasure" speech it would lead to questions about *why* he was practicing one, and then questions about why he hadn't bothered to practice one for Maddison. And then the whole thing would blow up in his face again, and Chris was tired of things blowing up in his face. And nothing had even blown up in his face literally; although with the way his life was going it was only a matter of time before something did.

Also, it was surprisingly difficult to come up with a "so we're searching for buried treasure" speech that wouldn't make someone panic. Maddison must just be unusually calm.

The Archer's Grove State Park was small, as far as state parks went, seeing as it was only a couple hundred acres of wetlands, swamp, beach, and interior vegetable tangle that was attractive to nesting seabirds, crocodiles, one very rare and very retiring species of mussel, and migratory flocks of tourists. It was also home to the coastal remains of several early attempts to settle the area, one of which, Dr. McRae explained over orange juice and carrot muffins at the picnic tables next to one of the major trailheads, was located just off one of the medium-difficulty hiking trails. It was this site that was the most likely place to look for the lost parish registry.

"Seeing as this is my area of expertise and all," he sighed as they pored over maps spread out over the picnic table.

"You could probably take a hiking trip that just happened to pass by it," Chris realized. "It'd be better to do it in two days, maybe three, but it's definitely doable. After Carrie's ankle gets better," he added. When he glanced up, intending to check how grumpy this was making Carrie, he discovered that Dr. McRae had a distant, wistful expression on his face. Then

Maddison looked up to see what Chris was looking at and Dr. McRae's look vanished.

"Dad?" Maddison asked.

"See, this is why I kept saying you should join the school newspaper," Dr. McRae told Maddison. "You don't even *like* hiking."

"I'm way too involved to back out now," Maddison said firmly. "And I'd rather see it through than ignore it, willingly or not."

Dr. McRae winced a little at that, as though she'd hit him with the pointed comment as well as Chris, but he did concede the point, and the conversation turned to Carrie's prognosis, which was good, with full mobility likely in the next two to three days. Chris didn't realize he'd wandered away from the picnic table until Maddison caught up to him on the edge of what could optimistically be called a beach on wet days and where he was flicking pebbles.

"Hey," she said.

"Hi."

"So," Maddison said. "I have two questions."

Chris nodded and waited.

"One," Maddison said, "when do you want to go look for possibly haunted ruins? And two," she said, "who the heck is Professor Griffin?"

"Um," Chris said, startled. "Well, Professor Griffin is an old family friend—he knew Aunt Elsie in college and they stayed in touch. He teaches oceanography at the college and partners with the Archive a lot. If you spend any time at Edgewater you've probably met him without realizing it. He's the tall blond guy who's always wearing a captain's hat?"

"Um," Maddison said, frowning. "I don't think so?"

Chris sighed. He loved Professor Griffin like a confusing but harmless uncle, and he didn't want to add to his absent-minded professor reputation, but he added, "He tends to walk into closed doors while he's reading his mail?"

"Oh! *Him.*"

"Yeah," Chris said. "He's less absent minded— or it doesn't matter as much that he's so absent minded—when he's in his element. He's *very* good at oceanography. I was actually going to tell him some of what we've been doing."

"You trust him that much?" Maddison asked.

"I've known Professor Griffin since I was a baby," Chris explained. "He was Aunt Elsie's best friend. I think he'd really want to help, plus he has a boat."

"Oh, I see."

"No, it's not like that. I mean kind of, that is—"

"I'm teasing you," Maddison said. "But Chris—when you mentioned him at the rectory the day before yesterday?"

"Yeah?"

"Okay, so my dad has this blank face he does when he can't decide how to respond to a situation," Maddison said, and she must have seen that Chris wasn't following her because she went on. "Like for example, when I was four I got into the art supplies when nobody was watching and put a line of handprints along all four living room walls, but I did it in a color that complemented the rest of the room and it looked like someone did it on purpose. And Dad walked in and saw me and got this utterly blank look on his face because he knew I'd been misbehaving but I'd accidentally made everything better, right?"

"Okay, I see," Chris said.

"He got that face again when you brought up Professor Griffin. And I don't have any idea why."

"Because they're colleagues, of a sort?" Chris suggested. "Where did your dad go to school?"

"That would be one of the many things he refuses to tell anyone," Maddison said, picking up a rock and tossing it.

"I'll avoid mentioning your dad to Professor Griffin until we find out why he made faces, then," Chris said. "It's probably just because he saw Professor Griffin walk into a door too many times, people get weird about that."

"True," Maddison said. "And dad *was* slowly dying of cat allergies, so I could have been misreading his expressions."

"And as for the other question," Chris added.

"Don't you and Carrie determine that? I don't have a summer job to worry about."

"Carrie and I kind of already asked Mrs. Hadler if she would mind us skipping a day or so next week," Maddison explained. "And it turns out she's going on vacation with her grandkids for the next two weeks. Starting Tuesday. She was just waiting for her book club's tea to be over."

Well in *that* case.

"So, do you want to go hiking this week, say, Monday through Wednesday?"

"I thought you'd never ask," Maddison said. "And then I thought you'd never tell, either," she added, which Chris could admit he deserved.

"That little comment about seeing it through rather than ignoring it was for me, wasn't it?"

"Well, you and dad, who is *still* worried about something he can't figure out how to tell me," Maddison said. She found a respectable skipping stone among the gravel and got a good three hops out of it before it sank. "And now he's decided to *also* worry about me dating, which is silly, because . . . "

"You're not, and we're not, and we probably won't ever if I don't grow out of the habit of keeping secrets?" Chris offered, and was surprised to find that it didn't even hurt very much.

"Chris," Maddison said patiently. "Sending an apology for being cryptic *in code* is not romantic."

"Um."

"I didn't even know what kind of cypher it was," Maddison added, and it shouldn't have made Chris so happy that she knew it was a cypher.

The cemetery was quiet, and deserted, and it being just past midnight this wasn't an odd occurrence. In a quiet corner near a statue of a weeping angel, a bouquet of asters rustled in the light breeze and shone in the light of a nearly full moon like tiny silvery stars. Or at least, they did until a shadow fell over them and plunged the grave of Elsie Kingsolver into inky blackness.

"You always did look good in moonlight," the man casting the shadow said. He was tall, and wearing a dark hooded sweatshirt that hid his face, and feeling— although he wasn't about to admit it to anyone, except perhaps the dead, who don't tell tales nor make you take a nap—overwhelmed.

"And there was some silly poem from an old werewolf film you liked, about the moon all bright and white, and the one"—he sighed, and sat down on the grass before the grave—"about the moon in the sky, and the tears in my eye, and all the world's moonlight can't lead me to you." He laughed. "And bless us all and curse the day I ever heard the name *San Telmo*," he finished. This wasn't actually how the rhyme went, but he didn't care.

"Because call me a liar if you want, but they might actually find it," he continued, plucking clovers from the grass in front of him with fast, skilled fingers. "They've gotten further in two weeks than we did in two *years,* and that's *with* you-know-who dogging their every footstep."

He was now wrapping clover stems together.

"He's gone and *insinuated* himself, the *jerk*," he said, conversationally. "Got the kids to trust him. It's enough to make you *bite* someone, Elsie, and that someone might just be him, and then won't work the next morning be awkward?"

He tucked in a few green stems and poked a last flower or two into some of the empty spaces, and a delicate flower crown lay in his lap, woven entirely from clovers. He took the old, wilted flower crown and tossed it into a nearby tuft of ornamental grass, where it would be able to decompose in peace. Then he pulled three of the asters from their bouquet and twisted them into the crown as a finishing touch, and laid the completed flower crown at the base of the headstone.

"At some point," he said, hauling himself to his feet, "I'll get out of this terrible habit of haunting graveyards like some sort of ghost. But, well, secrets. So it won't be anytime soon. So"—he started to turn away, and then abruptly turned back—"you'd be proud of them, Elsie," he said, honestly but reluctantly, after standing before the grave for a long moment. "Chris and Carrie and even Maddison McRae. Proud and a little unnerved, and Carrie looks *so* much like you at that age. You'd be unnerved, and very frustrated, and very worried . . . " He sighed. "But very, very proud."